Randy Scouse Gits
The Sex Lives of The Beatles

Danny Friar

For Angie, who always did like the juicy bits.

Danny Friar
Randy Scouse Gits: The Sex Lives of The Beatles

© 2013 Danny Friar
Self publishing

(life_in_albion@hotmail.co.uk)

ALL RIGHTS RESERVED. This book contains material protected under International and Federal Copyright Laws and Treaties. Any unauthorised reprint or use of this material is prohibited. No part of this book may be reproduced or transmitted in any form or by any means, electronic or mechanical, including photocopying, recording, or by any information storage and retrieval system without express written permission from the author.

While every effort has been made to ensure accuracy, the author cannot accept responsibility for any errors or omissions. So There.

Contents

Acknowledgments **9**

Introduction **12**

Chapter One: Winston Churchill! **16**

Chapter Two: Hello Little Girl **28**

Chapter Three: Hamburg Nights **51**

Chapter Four: Beatle Babies **75**

Chapter Five: Spanish Love Affair **104**

Chapter Six: Polythene Pam **121**

Chapter Seven: Norwegian Wood **156**

Chapter Eight: Fuck Day **171**

Chapter Nine: The Ballad of Linda and Yoko **198**

Chapter Ten: Wife Swap **210**

Chapter Eleven: Another Girl **224**

Chapter Twelve: Was John Lennon Gay? **252**

Special Thanks **258**

Acknowledgments

While researching this book the author has used a variety of different books including but not excluding: The Beatles Anthology by The Beatles, The Beatles: The Authorised Biography by Hunter Davis, The Quarrymen by Hunter Davis, Lennon in America: 1971-1980, Based in Part on the Lost Lennon Diaries by Geoffery Giuliano, The Lives of John Lennon by Albert Goldman, The Beatles in Hamburg by Ian Inglis, The Beatles in Hamburg: The Stories, the Scene and How It All Began by Spencer Leigh, Imagine This: Growing Up With My Brother John Lennon by Julia Baird, John, Paul, George, Ringo and Me : The Real Beatles Story by Tony Barrow, The Beatles Encyclopaedia by Bill Harry, The John Lennon Encyclopaedia by Bill Harry, The Paul McCartney Encyclopaedia by Bill Harry, The George Harrison Encyclopaedia by Bill Harry, The Ringo Starr Encyclopaedia by Bill Harry, The Man Who Gave The Beatles Away by Allan Williams and William Marshall, Paul McCartney: Many Years From Now by Barry Miles, Woman: The Incredible Life of Yoko Ono by Alan Clayson, Barb Jungr and Robb Johnson, Loving John: The Untold Story by May Pang and Henry Edwards, A Secret History by Alistair Taylor, John by Cynthia Lennon, The Beatle Who Vanished by Jim Berkenstadt, The Beatles' Shadow: Stuart Sutcliffe and His Lonely Hearts Club by Pauline Sutcliffe and Douglas Thompson, Fab: An

Intimate Life of Paul McCartney by Howard Sounes, John Lennon: Living On Borrowed Time by Frederic Seaman, John Paul & Me: Before The Beatles by Len Garry, Alma Cogan: A Memoir by Sandra Cogan, Standing In The Wings: The Beatles, Brian Epstein and Me by Joe Flannery and Mike Brocken, Body Count by Francie Schwartz, Magical Mystery Tours: My Life With The Beatles by Tony Bramwell, I'll Never Walk Alone: An Autobiography by Gerry Marsden and Ray Coleman, Be My Baby: How I Survived Mascara, Miniskirts, and Madness, or My Life As a Fabulous Ronette by Ronnie Spector, What's it All About? by Cilla Black, Ringo Starr: Straight Man or Joker by Alan Clayson, The John Lennon Letters by Hunter Davis.

A number of newspaper articles and magazine articles have been used including but not excluding: The Observer, The Sunday Times, Liverpool Echo, Sunday Mirror, Beatles Book Monthly, The Sun, The LA Times.

Other sources of research include; John Lennon's audio diary and various interviews with members of The Beatles and their inner circle, wives, and girlfriends as well as conversations between the author and Ruth McCartney, Pete Best, Roag Best, Colin Hanton, Rod Davis, Julia Baird, Allan Williams, Joe Flannery and Brittnay Starr.

Special thanks to Pete Nash who answered some puzzling questions.

Introduction

Since the early 1960s every man and his dog have written about a rock group from Liverpool that made it big. For nine years they ruled the pop charts, they had 18 UK number one singles, and 11 UK number one albums. They played to sold-out audiences across the globe, they have sold billions of records, they have made history, they are untouchable, they are, of course, The Beatles.

In this book I am not going to tell the story of The Beatles, it has been told hundreds of times before. Most people already know their story-it's now taught in our schools and we all know their songs. There's nothing much else to say. Or is there?

In my collection of over two hundred books on The Beatles, I have books on The Beatles' fashion, instruments, film footage, radio appearances, business dealings, religious beliefs, philosophy, unreleased music, comic strips, and press reports...I even have some on The Beatles' music!

Sex is one of the few things The Beatles and their inner circle have shyed away from in interviews. It is one of the few things that hasn't yet been written about in great detail and why would it be? After all we are British. Sex is still a very taboo subject in Britain. We'd much rather have a cup of tea, thank you very much.

Even John Lennon, the most outspoken of the fab four, has had very little to say when it came to the sex lives of Britain's best loved sons. Over the decades since The Beatles split in 1970, more and more stories have surfaced, more and more secrets have come to light. This book sets out to tell those stories for the first time, to tell the story of The Beatles like it has never been told before. This is the story of the fab four as it happened under the sheets.

The Beatles were born and raised in Liverpool, a port city in the North of England, and it shows. John, Paul, George, and Ringo were four very typical northern lads, they enjoyed sex and female company like any other lad brought up in the North of England. Unlike most northern lads, or lads from any other part of the country for that matter, The Beatles had women literally throwing themselves at them and they weren't going to turn down an opportunity like that. The Beatles were, to put it simply, and to slightly misquote the title of a song by The Monkees, randy scouse gits.

John Lennon once said that he wanted the world to see The Beatles with their trousers off. Randy Scouse Gits: The Sex Lives of The Beatles presents The Beatles with their trousers well and truly off.

If your image of The Beatles is that of clean-cut, nice polite lads that sang 'I Want To Hold Your Hand' then prepare to be shocked! Sex, drugs, and rock 'n' roll have always gone hand in hand. Rock 'n' roll is literally black American slang from the '40s and '50s that means sex. When artist like Elvis Presley, Little Richard, and Chuck Berry sang about 'Rockin' and Rollin'' with their girl they meant in the bedroom rather than on the dance floor. Even before Elvis shook his hips for the first time, people were singing songs about sex. (Blues singer Bessie Smith was singing about needing some sugar in her bowl and a hotdog in her roll back in 1931) And why wouldn't they be? People have been getting laid since the dawn of time, it's a part of everyday life, it's what keeps the human race going-without sex none of us would be here today. The average person has sex 103 times a year, so why not talk about it? The fact of the matter is musicians get 'it' a lot more than the average man or woman and The Beatles are no exception to the rule.

I am a fan of The Beatles and have been since before I can remember. I grew up on the music of The Beatles, my dad would play their music to me when I was just a little boy. Some of the first albums I owned were Beatle albums 'borrowed' from my dad's collection. I first became seriously interested in The Beatles in my teens and started building up my collection of albums and books. I began to increase my knowledge of the band and paid my first visit to Liverpool in August 2004. Since then I have been to the city over 30 times. I have visited many major Beatle sites across England including Abbey Road Studios, Penny Lane, Strawberry Field, The Cavern, and The Beatles' childhood homes among others.

I have met and had conversations with many people connected to the group including ex-Quarrymen Rod Davis and Colin Hanton, ex-Beatle drummer Pete Best and his brothers Rory and Roag, half-sister of John Lennon Julia Braid and step-sister of Paul McCartney Ruth McCartney, ex-Beatles manager Allan Williams, and former booking manager for The Beatles Joe Flannery.

I was on the set of Nowhere Boy for two days in March 2009. I have written regularly for the British Beatles Fan Club magazine since 2011 and since March 2013 I have written for newspapers across the UK and the Channel Islands on the subject of The Beatles, as well as writing for other magazines including Down Your Way and Beatlefan magazine.

I am in no way trying to bring The Beatles down or scandalise them. Many before me have tried and failed. I don't think it would be possible even if that was my intention-It's not. I'm simply trying to cover an aspect of their lives that has not yet been covered. This book is the result of years of research and I believe everything in this book to be true and to come from first-hand accounts.

1

Winston Churchill!

All four Beatles were born during the Second World War, a time when sex was taboo, out of wedlock births were frowned upon and, abortion and homosexuality were illegal. It was a long way from the swinging sixties, free love, and the pill.

Teenage boy's minds still worked the same way they do today and when a fifteen-year-old Alfred Lennon and his friend stepped into Sefton Park one weekend in 1927 they had only one thing on their minds. Dressed in his finest suit topped off with a bowler hat and cigarette holder, Alfred was out to pick up girls. He spotted a young Julia Stanley, then fourteen, sat on a wrought-iron bench. Alfred had seen her before at the Trocadero club, a converted cinema on Camden Road, and thought she looked "lovely." Julia on the other hand thought he looked "silly" and told him to take his hat off. Alfred obliged and threw his hat into the lake. The two became friends and in December 1938 they married at the Bolton Street Register Office for a dare.

They spent their honeymoon at Reece's restaurant in Clayton Square and then went to the cinema. The newlyweds spent their wedding night separated-Julia went back to her family home while

Alfred returned to the boarding house he was staying at. Shortly after the wedding, Alfred signed up to the Merchant Navy working as a bellboy on a ship bound for the Mediterranean. It's unknown if Alfred ever cheated on Julia while at sea but it would be no big surprise as sailors were known for having a girl in every port, and if it wasn't a regular girlfriend, it was a prostitute. Sailors like Alfred were known for indulging in the services of certain ladies of the night and sang about them in their shanties.

Julia, on the other hand, wasn't going to sit at home and wait for her husband to return. While Alfred was away at sea, Julia, an attractive, slim twenty-five-year-old red head was out having a good time. She enjoyed dancing and singing and was very much a party girl. Then in January 1940, after one of Alfred's returns to Liverpool, she found herself pregnant. Alfred would later claim that the baby had been conceived on the kitchen floor of 9 Newcastle Road-Julia's parents' home where she lived at the time.

On 9 October 1940, she gave birth to a baby boy she named John Winston Lennon. His father, Alfred, was away at sea at the time and John later quipped that he had been born "out of a bottle of whisky" which pretty much sums up his parents' relationship. In 1942, Julia moved out of the family home and moved into a dairy cottage on Allerton Road owned by her brother-in-law, George. Julia began going out again and a local girl was hired to baby-sit John. It wasn't long before Julia's sister, Mimi, found out about Julia's nights out at the dancehalls and she wasn't best pleased. Mimi told Julia that she should be staying in at night and looking after John herself but Julia loved the night life and had become popular at the local pubs and dancehalls. She wasn't going to give it up for anything and, not wanting to be caught out, she stopped using the babysitter and started leaving John at home on his own.

American G.Is arrived in Britain in 1942, with the first batch arriving in Liverpool at the beginning of 1943. Before then, England was a drab and dreary place and the G.Is helped to spice things up a bit. For a lot of women in Liverpool it was the first time they would have met and even slept with a black man. Black people had been living in Liverpool since the 18th century but it wasn't until the arrival of the G.Is that the black population increased. As Julia became more and more popular at the local pubs and dancehalls, she no doubt became popular with the American G.Is that frequented them. It's quite possible that on more than one occasion Julia took a handsome young yank back to the cottage. After all, Americans were exotic, (Julia loved going to the cinema and fell in love with everything American) handsome, rich, and could provide items such as Nylon stockings, cigarettes, Coca-Cola, chocolates, and candy. Julia wouldn't have been alone in having a relationship with an American G.I. Around 70 thousand British women became G.I brides with over 6, 500 of those marrying G.Is from the Butonwood base in Warrigton (around 20 miles from Liverpool). 20 thousand babies were born in Britain to G.I fathers but it wasn't just the Americans that caught the attention of the Liverpool lassies.

On one night out, Julia met a Welsh soldier named Taffy Williams. She began having an affair with him and in late 1944 she became pregnant. Later, Alf would blame himself for the affair because he had written a letter to Julia telling her to enjoy herself while the war was on. Little did he know she was doing just that.

When Alfred returned to Liverpool, at the end of 1944, he found his wife pregnant with another man's child. Julia claimed she had been raped by an unknown soldier. Alfred and his brother, Sydney, managed to track down Taffy, who was stationed in the barracks at Mossley Hill. Taffy told the two men his side of the story and all three of them returned to the cottage where they confronted Julia. Julia confessed to the affair and Alfred offered to raise the child as his own. Taffy offered to raise the child too but only if Julia gave up John. Julia turned down both offers and ended her relationship with both men. In June 1945, she gave birth to a baby girl at Elmswood Nursing Home. The girl was named Victoria Elizabeth Lennon. Under pressure from her family, Julia had to give Victoria up for adoption and the little girl was adopted by a Norwegian Salvation Army Captain, Peder Pedersen and his wife

Margaret, who renamed her Ingrid Marie Pedersen. John Lennon found out about his secret half-sister years later and tried to track her down but was unsuccessful. Nobody knew the whereabouts of Ingrid Pedersn until 1998 when she contacted the Liverpool Echo with her story. Ingrid had come across her true identity in 1966 when she found her adoption paper in a tin box owned by her mother. "I burst into tears" she remembers. She kept her identity a secret until the death of her mother in 1998.

After the birth of Victoria and with Alfred away at sea again, Julia began a second affair with another man. John Dykins was a good-looking, well-dressed wine steward at the Adelphi Hotel. Through his involvement in the local black market, John, known as Bobby, could provide Julia with luxury goods that were rationed at the time. He would give Julia gifts of alcohol, chocolate, silk stockings, and cigarettes. The couple soon moved into a flat in Gateacre together and for a while John lived with them. The one bedroom flat was not the ideal place to raise a family. There was only one bed that was shared by all three of them and as the infant John slept, his mother and her boyfriend would discreetly make love, trying not to wake up John. The Stanley family were not happy about Julia "living in sin" and Mimi took John to live with her at her house on Menlove Avenue.

Mimi was a very traditional woman when it came to family, sex, and relationships. Or at least she liked to think she was. She met her husband, George Smith, in 1932 while she was working as a nurse. George delivered milk to the hospital where she worked and they started courting. In 1939, they finally married and they bought a semi-detached house called Mendips in Woolton, a middle-class area of Liverpool. Mimi was 36 when she married and still a virgin. The couple never consummated their marriage and Mimi was still a virgin when George died in 1955.

Mendips had three bedrooms and during the 1950s the Smiths started taking in student lodgers. In September 1951, a nineteen-year-old bio-chemistry student at Liverpool University called Michael Fishwick moved into Mendips. He lodged at Mendips on and off for nine years, staying there during term time and when he returned in the autumn of 1955, he returned to a very different Mendips. George Smith had died of a liver haemorrhage in July 1955 and now only Mimi and a teenage John Lennon were living in the house. During that term Michael and Mimi developed a close friendship and by 1956 they had become lovers. Mimi lost her virginity to Michael in the bed she had once shared with her husband. Mimi, who was then 50, had told Michael she was 46, Michael was 24. The love affair continued right into 1960 and at one point the couple even discussed moving to New Zealand together but nothing came of it.

John Lennon was interested in sex from an early age. "I knew everything when I was about eight" he once told a reporter. He had learnt about sex from the graffiti on public toilet walls, pornographic images, and from his gang of friends. Sexual knowledge was passed on by word of mouth from one eight-year-old boy to another. As a boy, John would write poetry and wrote a lot of nonsense poetry in the style of Lewis Carroll. He once tried his hand at an erotic poem, "The sort you read to give you a hard-on" as he once put it. He wrote it and then hide it under his pillow. One day, while tidying his room, Mimi found it and was disgusted. When he got home from school that afternoon he was in trouble. John lied his way out of it saying he had been made to write it out by another boy who couldn't write very well.

John's uncle George had taught him his first rude poem which John, in turn, taught his best friend, Pete Shotton:

> In the shade of the old apple tree
> Two beautiful legs I can see
> And up at the top there's a little red dot
> It looks like a cherry to me
> I pulled out my private New York
> It fitted in just like a cork
> I bet you ten quid she'll be having a kid
> In the shade of the old apple tree.

Meanwhile, Julia and John Dykins had had two daughters together; Julia (born 1947) and Jackie (born 1949). Julia would never divorce Alfred and was living out of wedlock with Dykins and the two girls. Mini was disgusted and tried to keep John away from "the house of sin", Julia, and her bastard children. Ironically, Mimi had been born before her parents had been married and was a bastard herself. By the time he was eleven, John was visiting his mother and her new family at their home at 1 Blomfield Road regularly, sometimes staying overnight.

One night, John walked into his mother's bedroom to find her giving a blowjob to John Dykins. In his 1979 audio diary he recalls he felt shocked "but not that shocked, I was probably into it myself". John would later admit to finding his own mother sexual attractive. In his 1979 audio diary he describes a time when he was fourteen and he laid on the bed with her and wondered to himself if he should make a move or not. In the end he put his hand on her breast. "It was a strange moment" he recalls. He goes on to say he wished he had taken it further "if she had allowed it".

Julia was run over and killed by an off duty policeman outside Mendips in 1958. She had been visiting Mimi and was on her way home when she was hit by the speeding car. She was 44, John was 17. John's fantasies of his mother would last him the rest of his life. In 1979 he was to remark "Maybe the game is to conquer it before you leave, otherwise you come back for more and who wants to come back just to come?"

John was musical from an early age and the first

instrument he learnt to play was the mouth organ. He also owned an accordion that he would play with one hand. In his early teens his mother taught him to play the banjo. One of the songs he learnt to play was 'Maggie May'-a folk song about a Liverpudlian prostitute who robbed sailors. The song, or as much of it as they could remember, was recorded by The Beatles in 1969 and released on the album Let It Be.

Liverpool, like most port cities of the time, was riddled with prostitutes. In the 1800s the city was famous for its ladies of the night. A guidebook from 1816 mentions the "spectacle of vice and misery in their lowest forms" when referring to Paradise Street. Among the famous prostitutes on Lime Street, Paradise Street, and the surrounding area were Jumping Jenny, Tich Maguire, Mary Ellen, "The Battleship", Cast Iron Kitty, Harriet Lane, "The Dreadnought", and Maggie May. Maggie May was reported to have lived at 17 Duke Street and had offered her services to seamen on Lime Street itself and in the American Bar in Lime Street which was popular with American sailors away from home looking for a good time.

It was Julia who bought John his first guitar and he would play banjo chords on that too before he learnt to play it probably. He started to learn songs by the rock 'n' roll greats and the first thing he learnt to play on guitar was 'Ain't That A Shame' by Fats Domino. John loved rock 'n' roll and he loved the double entendre in the lyrics. One of his favourites was 'One Night (Of Sin)' by Smiley Lewis which had the lyric "One night of sin is what I'm praying for". Elvis covered the song in 1958 but cleaned up the lyrics for a whiter audience. Once he saw Elvis Presley, John Lennon realised the best and easiest way to attract the opposite sex was to be on stage playing rock 'n' roll. In 1975 he was quoted as saying, "I thought of nothing else but rock 'n' roll; apart from sex and food and money - but that's all the same thing, really". At sixteen, John joined his first group, a skiffle group made up of his school friends called The Blackjacks. John soon took over as leader and the group became The Quarrymen.

John Lennon's gang of friends were wannabe Teddy Boys. They would dress like Teddy Boys but if they went into the tough districts of the city and came across real Teddy Boys, who were in their twenties and carried weapons, they would have to flee in fear of their lives. On their home turf however Lennon's gang was the toughest around. "The sort of gang I led" John told a reporter in 1967 "went in for things like shoplifting and pulling girls' knickers down." John's gang of friends would do everything together, even masturbate. According to his best friend at the time, Pete Shotton, John was eleven when he first boasted he could masturbate. Pete didn't believe him so the pair went into the garage of Pete's house and John showed him how it was done. Pete tried, but he couldn't manage to reach a climax. Once Pete had got the hang of it, a few months later, the pair would masturbate in the bushes on their way home from school.

"We'd also get the gang together" Pete told author Hunter Davis "for mutual wanking sessions." These sessions would take place in the park, where the gang would gather around and John would shout out the name of someone they all fancied. One of the biggest crushes the lads had was the French actress Briditte Bardot. John had her poster on his bedroom ceiling above his bed which he would stare at while he masturbated on the bed. Once the name had been called they all would begin to masturbate to see who could come first. According to Pete, John would come very quickly and almost always won. One time, John decided to shout out 'Winston Churchill!' Try as they might, none of the teenage boys could manage to reach a climax for laughing.

Not only could John come very quickly, but he could also get an erection again very quickly too. Pete once challenged him to do it ten times in a row. Pete told him if he could manage it he could watch the family's TV for as long as he liked. Pete was the first in his street to own a TV, something John's family didn't have the luxury of owning. John managed nine times but couldn't make it to ten.

John's other teenage fantasies included Anita Ekberg, the Swedish actress and model, and French actress and singer Juliette Greco. "I'd always had a fantasy about a woman who would be a beautiful, intelligent, dark-haired, high-checkboned, free-spirited artist a la Juliette Greco" he told one reporter in 1978. John's fantasy, in his opinion, came true when he met Yoko Ono.

2

Hello Little Girl

John Lennon was fourteen when he lost his virginity, making him the first of his group of friends. Pete Shotton remembers John bragging about it after. "I've just had my first screw" he told his best friend on the corner of Menlove Avenue and Vale Road. "It was a hell of a job getting inside. It was like trying to get it into a mouse's ear 'ole." he complained before adding "Actually, I'd rather have a wank".

The other boys in John's gang were still struggling to get a girl to go the whole way. A few of them had experienced what John would later call 'edge-of-the-bed-virgins'-girls who would go most of the way but never would sleep with you. Luckily, the lads knew a secret; if you went to the Abbey Cinema near Penny Lane and went to the back of the balcony you'd find two girls sitting together. According to Pete's friend Billy Turner you could touch them up and they wouldn't complain. Pete didn't believe him and went to check it out. It was true and he told John. John didn't believe it either and so one Saturday afternoon he and Pete went together. John and Pete sat at the back with one girl each. They fondled the girl's breasts and put their hands up the girl's knickers. "It was amazing" Pete recalls. "A dream come true. Naturally, you'd come in your pants."

Another of John Lennon's friends was Len Garry. Len would become the tea-chest bass player in the Quarrymen. One day, he and John were chatting up two girls that they had been following around Reynolds Park, Barbara and Miranda. The boys both fancied Barbara and asked her who she liked best. Barbara liked Len the most and the two started going out. Len told John if things didn't work out he could step in. A few weeks later, John did just that and Barbara became John's first regular girlfriend.

Barbara Baker was a fourteen-year-old glamorous strawberry blonde who lived on Ridgetor Road. She attended Sunday school at St Peter's Church in Woolton, as did John and his friends. She was a pupil at Calder High School and she would go out with John for over a year. John would write pages of love poems and give them to her but that's where the romance stopped. When the couple slept together for the first time John couldn't wait to tell his best friend Pete. One day John took Barbara to a graveyard where he had sex with her on a gravestone. "My arse got covered in greenfly" he recalled in 1978.

Mimi didn't allow John to bring girls back to Mendips so John would take Barbara to Pete Shotton's house so that they could make love. Pete and his girlfriend and John and Barbara would go up to Pete's bedroom and the two couples would make love, sometimes they would even share the same bed. Other times, the foursome would go to Pete's girlfriend's house. One day, the four teenagers sat in the girl's living room waiting for her mother to leave. Once the girl's mother left the room to cook their tea, John and Barbara started kissing on the sofa. Pete's girlfriend pulled down her knickers and straddled Pete in his chair. Suddenly, they heard a knock on the door. "Come in" John shouted, quickly zipping up his trousers. The girl's mother came in, "tea's ready" she said. John jumped up and grabbed hold of Pete's arm and pulled him from the chair where he had been trying desperately to lose his erection. "C'mon Pete!" he said "What's the matter with you?"

Barbara would often call round to Mendips but Mimi would tell her John was out. She would then walk to Blomfield Road and wait outside Julia's house. Some days she would wait for hours at a time to see John. One day, she called over John's half-sister, Julia, and asked her to get John to come outside. Julia ran inside and passed on the message but John just groaned and asked his mother to go out and tell her to go away. John's mother marched to the front gate and called out "What is it you want, dear?" Embarrassed, Barbara turned and ran off with Julia and her younger sister, Jackie, chasing after her. When the two girls caught up with Barbara she begged them to ask John to meet her. This time John came out, the couple embraced and kissed before climbing over an old stone wall and disappearing in the long grass leaving Julia and Jackie giggling on the other side. John popped his head over the wall and told the girls to leave but they wouldn't. In the end he had to bribe them with a half crown.

John left Barbara for a while and started seeing a girl called Margaret Jones. Margaret had also gone out with Len Garry and while Len was dating Margaret, Billy Turner was dating her friend, Beryl Woods. After Billy and Beryl broke up, Billy began seeing Barbara behind John's back. John was fuming when he found out but Billy and Barbara only lasted a few weeks and soon Barbara and John were back together. Despite Barbara's parents and John's Aunt Mimi trying to separate the couple they stayed together thought out the first year of Art College but by the second year they had both started to see other people.

Paul McCartney joined the Quarrymen in 1957, after meeting John Lennon at the Woolton Village Fete at St Peter's Church. Paul, then fifteen, was born James Paul McCartney on 18 June 1942 at Walton Hospital. His father, Jim, was working as a volunteer firefighter during the Second World War and his mother, Mary, was a midlife. They met in 1940 during an air raid and they married in April 1941 at St. Swithin's Roman Catholic chapel in Gillmoss, West Derby. Jim was 38 and Mary was 32. A second son, Michael, was born in 1944. In 1955, the family moved into 20 Forthlin Road in Allerton where they lived until 1964. A year after moving into the house

Mary died of breast cancer leaving Jim to raise the two boys by himself. That year Paul was given his first musical instrument, a trumpet, which he later traded it in for a guitar. He was a quick learner and soon not only could he play the instrument but he wrote his first song, 'I Lost My Little Girl', about the death of his mother. He also learnt to play piano and at sixteen he wrote the tune that would become 'When I'm Sixty-Four'. John too was writing songs. His first being 'Hello Little Girl'.

Paul had had a few girlfriends before joining the Quarrymen but hadn't got very far. At thirteen he would draw pictures of nude woman and keep them in his shirt pocket. When he was caught by his parents, like John with his poem, he blamed another boy but, after a grilling from his father, he admitted to it. One of his earliest girlfriends was a young girl called Linda Thorpe who lived on Forthlin Road. "When I first met Paul" she later recalled to a reporter "we used to shine lights at each other from his bedroom at the front to my one - I was in the front as well." The two teenagers would shine the lights as a way of saying goodnight after spending the day together. Another girl, Sheila Prytherch, lived at 8 Ardwick Road. The couple would hold hands and kiss. Paul was her first kiss. "It was innocent and lovely" she remembers. They went to the cinema one afternoon and Paul told her he could sing better than Frank Sinatra.

Another of his girlfriends was a girl with long beautiful hair called Val. Paul had first noticed her on the bus to school. One night, word got to Paul that Val liked him too. "You should have seen the way he went on!" says his younger brother, Michael. Paul took Val on a few dates to the cinema and to visit friends but after a few weeks their relationship fizzled out. Paul's next girlfriend was an older girl called Layla. "Which was a strange name for Liverpool" Paul would tell author Barry Miles. Layla would ask Paul to help her baby-sit. Baby-sitting was a great opportunity for a young teenage boy to get his leg over as the two lovers would have the house to themselves for a few hours. However, they would have to listen out for the key turning in the front door "because if you were caught with your pants down, that would be the ultimate disgrace" Paul told author Barry Miles but luckily for Paul, he was never caught but admits he came close to it more than once. It was with Layla that Paul lost his virginity at the age of fifteen. The next day, he couldn't wait to get to school to tell his friends. Another of Paul's early girlfriends was Julie Arthur, who was the niece of Liverpudlian comedian, Ted Ray.

When Paul was sixteen he started dating a girl called Celia. Celia was an art student about the same age as Paul and on one date she had with him John tagged along. John was under the impression Paul was meeting him that day. Paul, on the other hand, thought he had cancelled on John. None the less John was a mate so Paul let him come along. At the end of the night Celia asked Paul why he'd brought along "that dreadful guy." Paul's response was "Well, he's all right really". Their relationship didn't last much longer.

John's next girlfriend after Babara was an art student called Thelma Pickles. She first met John Lennon in 1958 when she became a student at Liverpool College of Art. A mutual friend, Helen Anderson, introduced the pair. Thelma was sixteen, John was a little bit older at seventeen. Thelma remembers "My first impression of John was that he was a smartarse." Wilfred Pickles was a radio presenter in the 1950s and when John heard Thelma's name he asked "Any relation to Wilfred?" Thelma, of course, had heard that one a thousand times before.

John's mother had died during the summer holidays and news of her death had got around the college. Suddenly, a girl called across the room "Hey John, I hear your mother's dead". Thelma felt sick. She had lost her mother just two months before. John didn't even flinch, he simply replied "Yeah". "It was a policeman that knocked her down, wasn't it?" the girl asked. Again, John didn't react "Yeah, that's right" he replied. Thelma was impressed by his braveness. At the end of the day neither of them were in a rush to get home. They sat talking together on the steps of the Queen Victoria monument near the bus terminal. They soon found they had a lot in common and a friendship blossomed.

Thelma had assumed that John lived with his father but one day he told her "My dad pissed off when I was a baby." This was something else the friends had in common. Thelma's father had left his family in 1951 when Thelma was ten. Thelma remembers that being from a broken home was something to be ashamed of. "You could never discuss it with anybody" she later recalled. It was this bound that brought the two closer together and by February 1959 they had become a couple.

Aunt Mimi still didn't allow girls into Mendips so, John and Thelma would meet up in a brick-built shelter on the golf course near John's home and wait for Mimi to leave. Once Mimi was out of the way, the couple would go into the house to spend some time together. The first time John took Thelma home he showed her around. "It seemed really posh to me, brought up in a council house." she remembers. They kissed and cuddled in the bedroom but before things could go any further Paul McCartney and George Harrison came round. The four of them had beans on toast and then the three lads played their guitars in the kitchen. Thelma had to leave early to avoid being caught by Mimi.

The couple started sagging off college to go on afternoon dates. They would spend time in a local pub, Ye Cracke on Rice Street or go to the cinema to see horror films. One afternoon, Thelma and John went to see the Elvis film King Creole at the Odeon. John hadn't taken his glasses, he hated wearing them in public and throughout the movie he would tug on Thelma's hand and ask "What's happening now, Thel?" The couple continued to spend time at Mendips whenever Mimi was out. They would go up to John's room and make love. "We didn't call it sex" Thelma remembers "that word wasn't really used by people then". Instead, John called it "going for a five-mile run". The couple never used protection and it was by sheer luck that Thelma never got pregnant.

Thelma was a bit of a toughie who shared and enjoyed John's dark humour and his often cruel wit, for a while at least, but John proved to be too much for her. "I will have to be a lot older before I can face in public how I treated women as a youngster" he said years later. The relationship ended in July 1959, when Thelma temporarily left college. Thelma's absence effectively ending the relationship but they remained close friends. "It just petered out." Thelma remembers "I certainly didn't end it. He didn't either." John already had his eye on another girl, Cynthia Powell.

Meanwhile, George Harrison had joined the Quarrymen in March 1958. Born in 1943, he was the youngest son of Harold and Louise Harrison. He had a sister, Louise and two brothers, Harry and Peter. He was fourteen when he join the group, after auditioning upstairs at the back of a double decker bus one night. He played 'Raunchy'-an instrumental hit for Bill Justis the year before. His first girlfriend was a young girl called Jennifer

Brewer but their relationship was mere child's play. The two met in July 1955, while on holiday in Devon and, at the end of the holiday, they became pen pals. George was 12 and Jenny, as she was known, was around the same age. They met up the following year when George introduced Jenny to the music of Elvis Presley.

His first real girlfriend was twelve-year-old Iris Caldwell. Iris was the younger sister of Alan Caldwell, a singer who later became known as Rory Storm. Iris and George first met at the Palace Ice Rink on Prescot Road. George's friend, Arthur Kelly, had been on a date with a girl called Ann Harvey, and when he asked if he could see her again she told him "Only if you bring a friend for my friend." Arthur brought along George and Ann's friend turned out to be Iris Caldwell. It wasn't long before George would be round at Iris' house almost every night after school. Iris remembers George playing the guitar and even wanting to join Rory's group which was then called The Raving Texans. Rory turned him down saying he was too young. Iris remembered later "the main reason he went out with me was that he wanted to get in a group." Iris and George would spend time walking down Lilly Lane kissing and cuddling. "Which was like a lovers' lane" Iris remembers. George was the first boy Iris had ever kissed.

Rory Storm opened a skiffle club in his basement, which Iris couldn't go to because she was under 15. Not wanting to miss out on the action, she stuffed her bra with cotton wool and put blue blusher on her eyes to make her look older. It worked and Iris spent the night in the club. At the end of the night, Rory made a joke about his little sister having cotton wool down her bra. Embarrassed, Iris ran out in floods of tears. George went after her, put his arm around her and kissed her. Iris remembers George as being "the best kisser ever." Forty years later, George would still remember Iris as the girl with cotton wool in her bra. George remembered her brother Rory better and remembers him as being very sporty. "Rory was an athlete." he once said "I remember a couple of times I came to have a date with Iris, and Rory would come running up to his front door sweating and panting, and checking his stopwatch, because he'd been training." George was always visiting Iris at home and her mother, Violet, remembers them watching TV and holding hands at least three times a week. George would later downplay the relationship saying "She probably didn't ever think she was my girlfriend. You never know when you're young."

George and Iris were still seeing each other in 1959, when Iris turned fourteen. Violet remembers George turning up to the party in a brand new Italian-style suit covered with buttons. At the party, the teenagers played kissing games and George and Iris always ended up together. It was during one of these games that George insulted Iris' friends. The boys would leave the room and all the girls would be named after fruits. The boys would then come back in and be asked if they would like an apple or a pear. Whichever fruit was picked the girl named after it would get a kiss. When it came to George's turn he didn't find either of them attractive so, when asked if he wanted a pear or a lemon George replied, "I'm not hungry". Iris was upset and ended the relationship.

George's next girlfriend was an attractive and clever young girl called Ruth Morrison. The pair met in the summer of 1958, when George was playing with The Les Stewart Quartet. The Quarrymen weren't getting many gigs at time and George was an active member of both groups. The Les Stewart Quartet had been playing at the Lowlands Club in Heyman's Green but hadn't managed to get any other gigs. It was Ruth who told them to speak to Mona Best, who was about to open a new club called The Casbah.

The band spoke to Mona, who promised them they could play at the club once it had opened. Before the Casbah opened however, the group had a row and two of the members refused to play the gig. Not wanting to let Mona down, Ken and George decided to try and put together another group. George told Ken about two mates that he sometimes played with. George asked his two mates if they wanted to play the gig, they did and that night George turned up to the Casbah with John Lennon and Paul McCartney.

George continued to go out with Ruth for a little

while and they would hold hands, cuddle and kiss but nothing more. Not that George didn't try. At an all-night party at Pete Best's house, George remembers snogging Ruth and having an erection for eight hours "till my groin was aching" but he didn't get anywhere that night or any other night. "Those weren't the days" he said later. George's relationship with Ruth ended when she moved to Birmingham with her family.

At another party held by Les Stewart, at his house on Queen's Drive, George managed to pull a blonde girl with pigtails who was an art student and some years older than George. "She was cute in a Brigette Bardot sense" George remembered later. When John found out he was impressed and George remembers it as being "the first time I gained some respect from John."

Pete Best was born in Madras, India on 24 November 1941. His father, John, was a physical training instructor in the British army and his mother, Mona, was a nurse in the Red Cross. The family moved to Liverpool in 1944, after the birth of a second son, Rory. In August 1959, his mother opened the Casbah in her basement. A year later, after Mona bought him a drum kit, Pete joined The Beatles.

Paul's first long-term girlfriend was a shy, middle-class grammar school girl called Dot Rhone. Dot was a sixteen-year-old student at Liverpool Institute for Girls at the same time Paul attended

Liverpool Institute. Paul first met Dot in September 1959 at the Casbah Club in Hayman's Green, West Derby. The Quarrymen had played at the club on its opening night and were playing again that night. Two of the band members tried chatting up Dot that night. One was Paul, the other was John. It was John who won Dot over with his rugged looks but once she found out he had a girlfriend she went after Paul. As Dot spoke to Paul she said she needed some fresh air and asked him to join her outside in the garden. They kissed and arranged a date. They went to see a movie and after that night they began going out.

The couple would go to the cinema, the ballrooms or to see rock 'n' roll groups at various clubs and coffee bars in Liverpool. Dot later remembered feeling very special to be part of that scene. What made it more exciting for Dot was the fact that Paul was in a band and he had longish hair. Because of her work colleagues laughing and joking about Paul's hair she felt rebellious. "Whatever everyone else was doing, I always wanted to do the opposite" She said later.

One night at the Casbah, while Paul was rehearsing upstairs with the band, Dot was downstairs jiving with a boy she liked. When Paul came down stairs and saw the pair he was furious. He marched over to Dot with her coat in his hand. "We're going" he told her and left. Dot followed after him and that night the couple had their first row. Paul had become very possessive and controlling and had a set of rules Dot had to follow. "I feel ashamed to admit it now" she said in an interview in 1997 "but back then I went along with it." Dot wasn't allowed to see her friends and she wasn't allowed to smoke when she was with Paul even though he smoked himself. Paul wanted Dot to look like Bridget Bardot and insisted she always wore black and made her dye her hair blonde. One time, he even paid for her to have it done the way he wanted and made the appointment. When she came out she looked terrible. She hated it and so did Paul. He blamed her for letting the hairdresser do it that way. He told her "Give me a call when your hair grows" and walked off, not speaking to her for days after. Paul would buy Dot clothes to make her fit the image he had in his mind. He would buy her tight miniskirts and once, he bought her a black leather coat. "We got (Dot and Cyn) to go blonde and wear miniskirts. It's terrible really" Paul would later remember.

Dot was still a virgin when she met Paul and remembers "I had to fight him off" but she couldn't fight him off forever and one day when Paul had the house to himself he invited Dot over. Dot told her mother she was staying at a friend's house and sneaked round to Paul's house. Dot remembers being terrified that someone might come back and catch them at it but no-one did. Dot remembers Paul being "kind and gentle" and it was after that night that they became frequent lovers.

In February 1960, Dot found herself pregnant. She was a sixteen-year-old bank clerk, Paul was a seventeen-year-old musician still studying for his A-levels in English and Art at the Liverpool Institute. Dot's mother, Jessie, was disgusted. Jessie was a woman who very much cared what other people thought and there was no way she would allow her daughter to be seen walking the streets appearing pregnant. Dot felt she had no choice but to move in with her sister who lived in Manchester and have the baby adopted. Paul, however, refused to allow that to happen and said the two would raise the child together. Paul's dad, Jim, began planning a register office wedding-the couple didn't have much money for anything else. Everything was set, Dot and Paul were to marry, Dot would move in with the McCartneys and the two would raise the child together. Jessie still wasn't happy but Paul stood by Dot ensuring her that he would look after her. Jim needed ensuring too and told his son he would need a reliable full-time job in order to contribute to his new family's upkeep.

Three months into the pregnancy, Dot was rushed to hospital in an ambulance, she had suffered a miscarriage. Paul arrived at the hospital with flowers, he was clearly upset but Dot believes "deep down he was probably relieved." In hindsight she admits she too was relieved. A few months after her miscarriage, Paul and The Beatles set off to Hamburg for the first time.

Dot wasn't the only girlfriend that got left behind when The Beatles, as they were now known, went to Hamburg in August 1960. John had first met

Cynthia Powell at Liverpool College of Art in 1958. At the time he was dating Thelma Pickles. Thelma remembers Cynthia as being "dainty and sweet." "We used to take the mickey out of her" Thelma later admitted "but John always said he fancied her." Cynthia Powell was born in Blackpool on 10 September 1939, making her almost a year older than John. She was the youngest of three children. Her father, Charles Powell was a commercial traveller for the General Electric Company. He died of lung cancer when Cynthia was seventeen, the same age John was when he lost his mother. She enrolled into Liverpool College of Art in September 1957, when she was eighteen. Cynthia was from Hoylake, a middle-class area in the Wirral, and was considered to be posh. John and his friends would poke fun of her. "Quiet Please" John would shout "No dirty jokes. It's Cynthia!"

On the first day of the second year John introduced himself to Cynthia. Cynthia had seen him around but the two had never spoken before, despite Cynthia's attempts to get John to notice her. By half-way through the term, Cynthia started to fall for John. John would always have his guitar with him and one day he played 'Ain't She Sweet' to her. On the last day of term, before the summer holidays, a party was held in Arthur Ballard's classroom. Both John and Cynthia attended the party and John asked Cynthia if she wanted to dance. As they danced to Chuck Berry, John asked Cynthia "Do you fancy going out with me?" Cynthia turned him down. "I'm sorry" she told him "but I'm engaged to this fellow in Hoylake." "I didn't ask you to fuckin' marry me, did I?" John snapped before walking off. A few hours later, John asked Cynthia if she wanted to join him and his friends for drinks at Ye Cracke. Cynthia went to the pub with her friend Phyl but she was ignored by John and after a few drinks the two friends got up to leave. John teased her calling her a nun and asked her to stay. She agreed and after a few more drinks they left together.

Outside the pub, John kissed Cynthia for the first time. He whispered that his friend, Stuart Sutcliffe, had a room they could go to and, taking her by the hand, he led Cynthia down the road, buying fish and chips on the way. Stuart's flat was a mess. A mattress laid on the floor with clothes, empty cigarette packets and beer bottles, art materials, and books scattered around it. Cynthia and John climbed over the mess and made their way to the mattress where they made love for the first time. Cynthia had had sex before but it had only been very brief. She remembers this time lasted around an hour. After, as they held each other in their arms, John said, "Christ, Miss Powell, that was something else." He then asked her about her engagement and she told him that that relationship was over.

Realising the time, Cynthia and John quickly got dressed and rushed to the train station so Cynthia could get her last train home. They quickly kissed goodbye before Cynthia jumped onto the carriage.

"What are you doing tomorrow, and the next day, and the next?" John asked her as she waved out of the window. "Seeing you" she shouted back.

John and Cyn, as John was now calling her, didn't become a serious couple until a few weeks later. At the beginning of the summer holidays, Cyn and her mother Lillian had gone to visit her brother Charles in Buckinghamshire. Once she was back, Cyn spent all her spare time with John. They would sit in cafes for hours, making one cup of coffee last them as it was all they could afford. They would spend their evenings in Ye Crake, drinking pints of black velvet-a mix of Guinness and cider. If they could afford it they would go to the cinema, sitting in the back row kissing and cuddling. "We were always broke" Cyn said later "Our small daily allowances went on fares, lunch and, in John's case, the ciggies he smoked."

John wanted Cyn to put him first. He wanted to come before everything else including her college work, friends, and her mother. Cyn's college work started to slip even more when John insisted that they sagged off together. On warm days, they would get the ferry across the Mersey to New Brighton, where there was a funfair by the sea. Behind the beach, up on the deserted sand dunes, the couple would make love. They would get the ferry back with sand under their clothes. The young lovers would sit and giggle as they imagined what the other passengers would think if only they knew.

Like Paul with Dot, John became very possessive and controlling with Cyn. He wanted her to spend as much time with him as possible and would make her get the last train home. If she tried to get a train that wasn't the last train he would become angry and have a fit until he got his own way. He became very jealous and had noticed that Cyn had a few admires at college and would warn them off. "I was jealous of anyone she had anything to do with" he said in 1967. At one college party another student asked Cyn for a dance. Before she could answer, John had dived on the guy and had to be pulled off by a group of students. John also wanted Cyn to look like Brigitte Bardot and, like Paul had done with Dot, he got her to dye her hair blonde and wear miniskirts. "All my girlfriends who were dark-haired suffered my constant pressure to become Brigitte" John remembered in 1978.

Like all John's previous girlfriends, Mimi didn't allow John to have Cyn over and Cyn's mother, Lillian, wouldn't let John stay over either so, the couple had nowhere they could spend the night together. John would often talk Stuart into lending them his room for a few hours so they could have sex. When Stuart's room wasn't available, John would try to persuade Cyn into having quickies in dark alleys or shop doorways. Cyn never enjoyed these encounters so the pair stuck to kissing and cuddling anywhere and everywhere they could.

Although John and Cyn had been going steady for several months, John was still obsessed with ex-girlfriends and what may have been. When he was fifteen, one of John's very first girlfriends was a girl called Beth. They hadn't lasted long because Beth's parents, like that of many of John's early girlfriends, couldn't stand him and they put pressure on Beth to break up with John, which she did. Years later John was still thinking about her and would even mention her to Cyn but told her "don't worry, they've banned me from seeing her anyway, they think I'm a ruffian. They won't have me around". One evening, when he was meant to be meeting Cyn, John went to meet Beth instead. He wanted to see if he could make a go at it. Both Beth and John decided that night that it was long over and John returned to Cyn admitting where he had been the night before.

At an art school dance around Easter 1959, John tried to get back with Thelma Pickles. He took her to a darkened classroom where the two could be alone but it soon became obvious that they weren't the only ones who had had that idea. As the pair began kissing they heard giggles coming from the darkness. Thelma refused to do anything with other people in the room and went to leave but John grabbed her arm and pulled her back. He then hit her across the face. "Once he'd hit me that was it for me" Thelma said looking back in 2009.

Cyn too would be a victim of John's violent streak. One night at a party, John noticed Cyn dancing with his best friend and fellow art student, Stuart Sutcliffe. John, once again, lost his temper. The pair, noticing his rage, immediately stopped and Cyn rushed over to John and told him she loved him and no-one else. This seemed to have calmed him down but the next day at college John followed Cyn to the toilets in the basement. When she came out he was waiting for her. Without a word, he raised his arm and hit her across the face, knocking her head into the pipes that ran down the wall behind her. John then turned and left leaving Cyn feeling shocked and hurt. She had been left with no choice but to end the relationship.

For three months Cyn wouldn't speak to John. She avoided him whenever she could and she even went on a few dates with a local boy. John would remember the break-up years later saying, "She did leave me once. That was terrible. I couldn't stand being without her." One day, out of the blue, he phoned her and asked if she would come back to him. He apologised for hitting her and said it would never happen again. "I hesitated for a whole second before I said 'yes'." Cyn recalled in her book 'John'.

In early 1960, John moved in to Stuart's flat and at last he and Cyn had a place they could be alone together. It wasn't the most romantic of places and Cyn remembers a Belisha beacon and an empty coffin being part of the furniture. Around May of that year, the Quarrymen became The Beatles after Stuart and John stayed up all night thinking of a new name for the group. After many hours of nagging from John, Stuart bought a bass guitar and joined the group. In August, after Pete Best joined them on drums, The Beatles (John, Paul, George, Stuart and Pete) headed off to Hamburg, the city of sin.

3

Hamburg Nights

Stuart Sutcliffe was born in Edinburgh on 23 June 1940, making him the oldest of the group. His father, Charles, was a seaman and his mother, Millie, was a teacher. He had two younger sisters, Joyce and Pauline. He first met John Lennon at the Liverpool College of Art and the two became best friends. Stuart was considered the most talented student at the art college and one of Stuart's paintings was shown at the Walker Art Gallery in Liverpool as part of the John Moores exhibition, from November 1959 until January 1960. It was, in fact, only half of the painting. Stuart had dropped off the first canvas and had gone back to get the other half but was distracted on the way by John and ended up in Ye Crake. Nonetheless, Stuart's painting was bought for £65 by none other than John Moores himself. It is rumoured that Stuart used this money to buy a Hofner Pesident bass guitar but it has since been reviled that Stuart's guitar was paid for in instalments. Stuart was taught to play the instrument by another fellow art student called David May and joined The Beatles.

In May 1960, The Beatles, with Tommy Moore on drums, toured Scotland as Johnny Gentle's backing group. It was during that trip that the group got their first tastes of fame and life on the road. As they travelled from one town to the next, the group got to meet and sleep with local girls. Cyn had missed John during the two week tour and when he got back the pair couldn't wait to be alone together. Stuart went out for a few hours leaving the couple in the flat and they began making love. Suddenly, Cyn began to cry out in agony. She was suffering from a sharp pain in her abdominal. She begged John to take her home, they got dressed and headed to the train station where Cyn, in agony, crawled on to the train. Once she got home her mother called an ambulance and she was rushed to the hospital-she had appendicitis. A couple of days passed before John came to visit. Cyn had been desperate to see him but to her shock he turned up with George Harrison. When she saw George, Cyn burst into tears.

The group got the gig backing Johnny Gentle through Allan Williams, a club owner and booking agent on Merseyside, and it was through Allan that The Beatles got their next big break, four months playing the clubs in Hamburg. Before the band set off to Hamburg, John asked Cyn to go over to Mendips. Mimi had gone to visit her sister Nanny in Birkenhead. John had borrowed a camera and wanted to take some photos of Cyn to take with him to Hamburg. Cyn posed in various seductive poses, doing her best impression of Brigitte Bardot while John snapped away. After, they made love in Mimi's living room. Mimi was due back that evening and the pair decided they better leave before she got back. As they collected their belongings together the phone rang, it was Mimi: the buses weren't running because of bad fog and she wouldn't be home until morning. That night they slept together in John's single bed. The next morning Cyn left early not wanting to be caught by Mimi.

When John told Mimi The Beatles were going to play in Hamburg she wasn't at all pleased and she told him that he wasn't allowed to go. Unfortunately for Mimi, she had no say in the matter. John was almost twenty-years-old and was no longer living at home but Mimi had good reason to worry. Hamburg was known as the 'city of sin' and for good reason. "The whole area was full of transvestites and prostitutes" George would later remember. The five lads from Liverpool had never experienced anything like Hamburg and its red light district before. George Harrison, then only seventeen, was still a virgin.

Back in Liverpool, they had once backed a stripper called Janice. Janice was hired to appear at Allan Williams' New Cabaret Artists Club in June 1960. She refused to perform without a backing band so Allan paid The Beatles ten shillings each to back her. She gave them sheet music of Beethoven and Khachaturian but none of the group could read music and instead they played a selection of standards such as 'The Harry Lime Theme', 'September Song', 'Moonglow', 'Begin The Beguine', and 'It's a Long Way to Tipperary'. They backed Janice twice that night and as they played the lads watched the strip tease. "Everybody looked at her, just sort of normal" Paul remembers. At the end of the act Janice turned around to find four blushing red-faced lads. "We were all young lads" remembers Paul "We'd never seen anything like it before."

Paul began buying magazines like Parade to look at photos of nude women while sat on the top deck of the bus. For John and Stuart seeing a woman in the nude was no big deal. At Liverpool College of Art they would often draw and paint pictures of June Furlong, a nude artist's model. One day, when June was posing nude in front of the class, John waited for the teacher, Terry Griffiths, to leave. Once the coast was clear he jumped from behind his easel and sat on the model's knee. He began to grope her and the pair necked before John returned to his seat.

No amount of experience could prepare them for what was waiting in store for them in Hamburg. "We grew up in Hamburg" John once said "Not Liverpool." Hamburg's red light district was awash with all kinds of sex clubs, strip bars, and brothels. Prostitution was legal in Hamburg and down on The Reeperbahn girls would present themselves in the windows. George remembers "The Reeperbah and Grosse Feiheit were the best thing we'd ever seen, clubs and neon lights everywhere." Grosse Freiheit, the street that was home to three of the four clubs

The Beatles played at, means 'Great Freedom' and that is exactly what The Beatles experienced there.

They first began working at The Indra, a club owned by Bruno Koschminder, an ex-circus performer. The club was situated at Grosse Freiheit 64, just around the corner from the Reeperbhn. It had been a strip bar but its homosexual owner, Bruno, wanted to make it into a rock 'n' roll club which was more to his taste. When The Beatles arrived on the first night they watched the strip act. "We're not going to be backing strippers, are we?" they asked. "No" Bruno told them "Tomorrow is rock 'n' roll". The band would play mainly rock 'n' roll covers by the likes of Little Richard, Buddy Holly, Chuck Berry, and Elvis Presley.

It was in Hamburg that they experienced what we now call groupies for the first time. "We didn't call them groupies, then" John remembers "I've forgotten what we called them, something like 'slags'". The German woman loved the rough rockers from Liverpool and they would come and watch them play every night. Horst Fascher was then a twenty-four-year-old bouncer working on the door at the nearby Kaiserkeller when The Beatles first came to Hamburg. He claims part of their success was down to large numbers of women in the audience. "The girls were crazy about them" he recalls. All of The Beatles had left their girlfriends back in Liverpool and according to Rosemarie McGinnity, a barmaid at the Star-Club, The Beatles could have their pick of the German girls and they often did. "They took them for a blowjob, or what so ever" she remembers decades later. Some of the girls would have been prostitutes who offered their services for free. Paul's first Hamburg girlfriend was a girl called Corri Sentrop. Her family owned a restaurant next door to the Indra so Paul was able to get fed and laid. When interviewed in 1966 she remembered Paul as being a really good kisser and a gentleman.

The Beatles would take girls back to their digs in the back rooms of the Bambi-Kino, a pornographic cinema also run by Bruno. The five of them slept in the same room, an old storeroom next to the ladies toilets. The small room had pain concrete walls, there was no heating or windows and they had to sleep on bunk beds or camp beds with very thin sheets. "We were frozen" Paul remembers. There was no bathroom and the lads would have to wash in the cinema toilets. "We'd try to get into the ladies' first" John recalls "which was the cleanest of the cinema's lavatories"

Pete remembers how the lads would share five or six girls between them. As the band all made love at the same time they would call out to each other "How's yours going? I'm just finishing. How about swapping over?" One night the group had eight girls between them and legend has it that each Beatle slept with all eight of the girls twice.

Once John was in Hamburg, Cyn sent him more photos that she had taken in the Woolworths photo booth. Dressed in her most provocative outfit, she did her best sexy pose in the small booth and sent the end result to John, asking him for some photos in return. What she got back was not what she had been expecting. John was pulling faces at the camera and pretending to be a hunchback. "John could never play anything straight" Cyn remembers. Dot too had sent photos to Paul while he was away in Hamburg. He, in return, sent her publicity photos of the group taken in the Indra.

Hamburg was a city were anything was possible and for John and Stuart it was an artistic experience, the type they had read about in books. Since coming to Hamburg the two Liverpudlian men's attitude towards homosexual men had changed. In a letter Stuart wrote to his sister Pauline, back in Liverpool, he says that he had become popular "both with girls and homosexuals" but he insures her that he's not "keeping the company of homosexuals". "When in Liverpool" he writes "I would never have dreamt I could possibly speak to one without shuddering. As it is, I find the one or two I speak to more interesting and entertaining than any others".

John and Stuart began to wonder what it was like to have sex with another man. They wanted to experience anything and everything including each other. One day, Paul, George, and Pete went on a boat trip with some local girls leaving John and Stuart behind. The pair made their way around the various bars and clubs on the Reeperbahn. After hours of drinking the pair returned to the Bambi-Kino for a few hours' sleep before that night's gig. John took the bottom bunk leaving the top bunk for Stuart. The two started to discuss their sexual fantasies and before long John had crawled into bed with Stuart. According to John, Stuart gave him a blowjob but Stuart's sister, Pauline, thinks it more likely that it was the other way round.

In October, the Indra was closed down. An elderly woman had complained to the police that the noise of The Beatles was keeping her awake. Bruno was told he could either stop featuring live music or turn the Indra back into a strip club. Not wanting to go back to running a strip club, Bruno closed the club and The Beatles moved to the Kaiserkeller, a few doors down. The Kaiserkeller, also owned by Bruno, was a much larger and more popular club than the Indra. The Beatles were playing on stage for hours at a time and were finding it hard to keep going. A sixty-year-old toilet attendant called Rosa Hoffmann let The Beatles in on a secret-if you took preludin, a brand of German slimming pills, you could stay awake for up to six hours. As long as you kept taking the pills you could stay up all night, even for days at a time. The Beatles began taking these pills every night along with endless amounts of alcohol and amphetamines. Not only did the pills help them play for longer but it allowed them to make love for longer. Once The Beatles were off the stage they could be awake for a few hours longer with one of their German girlfriends.

All of the Beatles had German girlfriends during their time in Hamburg. The girls in Hamburg were nothing like the ones back home. In Liverpool you would have to get past girdles, corsets, and bras but in Hamburg "they were almost flashing it" remembers Paul. George even managed to lose his virginity. One night he took a girl back to the Bambi-Kino. She was a stripper who worked in one of the clubs in the area. In the dark room George thought he was alone with the girl. It wasn't until the pair had finished making love and three of the other Beatles (John, Paul and Pete) cheered that he realised they had been there all along. "At least they kept quiet whilst I was doing it" he said later looking back.

George wasn't the only one to sleep with a stripper in Hamburg. Pete had a girlfriend who worked as a stripper and whose husband was in jail. He would go back to her place where the pair could make love. Paul also had a stripper girlfriend. Before her Paul had not had many sexual experiences in his life. The stripper taught Paul a lot about sex in what he later called "a fairly swift baptism of fire into the sex scene." Paul also dated a barmaid called Liane. Lain Hines, a member of The Jets, was also working in Hamburg at the time and had become friends with Paul. When the Kaiserkeller closed at 2a.m Paul would go watch The Jets play their last set. Lain was dating Liane's friend Gerda and the four of them would go in Gerda's Volkswagen and drive to Liane's flat. They would cook hamburgers and listen to Everly Brothers records. The two musicians would make love to their girls before being driven back to the Reeperbahn.

One of the girls George was seeing was seventeen-year-old Monika Pricken. Monika first saw The Beatles playing at the Indra and took a liking to George. The two started dating and one day she invited the band back to her parents' house. "My parents always wanted to know who my friends were" she remembers. The family fed the hungry musicians and John played a medley of German and American hits in the family's living room. When George was deported from Hamburg for being under eighteen and working in the red light district after ten, Monika's mother made him a bag of sandwiches, fruit, and fruit juice. Monika and her friend, Helga, who was dating Pete for a time, took him to the train station where they saw him off, waving and crying.

Back in Liverpool, George's girlfriend was awaiting his return. Pauline Behan had first seen The Beatles playing at the Casbah Club and was first drawn to John but soon took a liking to George and the two started dating. While George was in Germany with The Beatles, Pauline had been out enjoying herself. One night, at a dance at the Orrell Park Ballroom, Pauline had been chatted up by the lead singer of another Merseyside group, Gerry Marsden of Gerry and The Pacemakers. That night, Gerry got Pauline's phone number but she made it very clear she was in a relationship with George. When

George returned to Liverpool, Gerry told him straight, "I've got some good news and some bad news. The good news is I'm in love" he said "the bad news is that it's your girl." The conversation didn't last long and Gerry left to tell Pauline he had ended the relationship for her. Despite Gerry's actions, George and Pauline continued going out but Pauline began seeing more of Gerry and one night when George rang Pauline, she told him she was very sorry but she had decided she would be happier with Gerry. Pauline and Gerry married in 1964.

John's Hamburg girlfriend was a young pretty girl called Renata. Renata was a German girl who lived near the Reeperbahn. She would come and watch The Beatles play at the Kaiserkeller. She was different from most of the girls in the audience because she wasn't a stripper or a prostitute, she was just a normal girl. She caught John's eye and in-between sets he would spend time with her. Unfortunately, Renata was under eighteen and due to a curfew which was enforced by local police she had to leave the club at ten o'clock. One night when the group went on stage they were missing a member. John was in the toilets with a girl (most likely Renata). The band began to play without him. Suddenly, John rushed out dressed in nothing but his underpants and a toilet seat around his neck.

Another visitor to the Kaiserkeller was a twenty-two-year-old artist, Klaus Voormann. Klaus had had an argument with his girlfriend, Astrid, and had gone for a walk to clear his head. He ended up on Grosse Freiheit where he heard rock 'n' roll music coming from the Kaiserkeller. He went inside and that night he watched The Beatles for the first time. The next night he returned and this time he was with his girlfriend, Astrid Kirchherr and best friend, Jürgen Vollmer. As soon as Astrid set eyes on The Beatles she decided all she wanted to do was to be as close to them as possible. "I had never seen boys that were that attractive before" she would later recall. Astrid Kirchherr was a beautiful, blonde, twenty-two-year-old photographer and during a break in The Beatles' set she spoke to the group and asked if she could take photographs of them. They agreed and the next morning they went to a nearby fairground where she took photos of the group posing in front of a truck. She became obsessed with The Beatles and John and Stuart became obsessed with her too. They would both write home about Astrid and Cyn soon became jealous thinking John was in love with Astrid. She was only half wrong.

Both John and Stuart tried it on with Astrid but in the end it was Stuart who won her over. Astrid left Klaus and began dating Stuart. Stuart was a very good looking young man who had a look of James Dean about him. He had had his fair share of girls back in Liverpool and would often draw or paint the girls he was seeing. One girl that he dated for several months was the subject of hundreds of sketches. Stuart was quite the romantic type and a bit of a perfectionist when it came to women. He was also quite the lover too and owned a copy of the Kama Sutra. Before Astrid however, Stuart hadn't shown much interest in the girls Hamburg had to offer because, as he put it, they were "lacking in quality".

Astrid and Stuart soon became inseparable. When the band were playing, Astrid would sit at the front of the stage, googling at Stuart the whole time. Once a night Stuart would hand his bass guitar to Paul and take centre stage. He would croon Elvis Presley's 'Love Me Tender' into the mike all the while not breaking eye contact with Astrid. Stuart began spending more and more time with Astrid and sometimes he would miss gigs. When The Beatles returned to Liverpool on 3 October 1960 Stuart stayed behind with Astrid.

The Beatles could leave their Hamburg girlfriends behind but they came back to Liverpool with a little reminder of their time there. Allan Williams remembers that most the bands that came back from Hamburg would have some form of STD. Although he won't name any names he does admit this included The Beatles. Little was known about STDs in the early sixties so the groups would go to Allan, a much older and wiser man, with their problems. Allan became known as 'The Little Pox Doctor of Hamburg'. He would examine the groin and penis, sometimes he would ask them to urinate into a glass and if he found anything unusual he would arrange for them to have private treatment.

John and Paul both wrote lengthy love letters to their girlfriends back in Liverpool but once they were back in Liverpool the tables had turned and now Paul was writing letters to the girls he had left behind in Hamburg. One day, Dot was in Paul's bedroom when she came across a postcard from a German girl. It had been written in English and she was saying she couldn't wait for Paul to come back to Hamburg. Dot was devastated but never said anything to Paul.

The Beatles returned to Hamburg in March 1961. This time they were to play at Top Ten Club at Reeperbahn 136. The club was owned by Manfred Weissleder but was being run by Horst Fascher who had been the bouncer at the Kaiserkeller the year before. Horst was a former featherweight boxer whose career ended after he was sentenced with manslaughter after accidentally killing a sailor in a street fight. Horst became friends with The Beatles and enjoyed a friendly back and forth with John. John would call him "a fuckin' Nazi" to which Horst would reply "fuck off, Limey". On their nights off Horst would show them around. The Beatles wanted to see everything the Reeperbahn had to offer and Horst was more than happy to show them.

The Beatles saw a lot on the Reeperbahn that they had never seen before. Strippers, transvestites and according to George, mud-wrestling women. There was also live sex shows. One legendry show, which The Beatles heard of but never saw, involved a woman and a donkey. One club on the Reeperbahn was Monika's Bar, a transvestite club. One night its owner, Monika, rushed over to the Top Ten club and told Horst that one of his 'boys' was at the club. When he asked who she replied it was one of The Beatles and told him to go have a look. Horst was intrigued and followed Monika back to the club where she told him to have a sneaky look. Horst ignored her and pulled back the curtain to reveal John Lennon receiving a blowjob from one of the transvestites. Ashamed, John quickly covered his privates with his hands but Horst told him not to worry as he had done the same before. According to Horst, "there was a transvestite who regularly used to give John blowjobs. When he found out she was a man, he was merely amused".

John wasn't the only member of the group to experiment with a transvestites. According to Allan Williams in his book, The Man Who Gave The Beatles Away, he met a Hamburg transvestite who claimed to have slept with two of The Beatles. To this day Allan will not reveal which two members of the group were mentioned. Another night, the group were visited by a friend from Liverpool called Bernie. That night they took Bernie to a club called the Roxy, another transvestite club. The Beatles had been there before but hadn't realised it was a transvestite club at first. Some of the transvestites in the club had taken a shine to The Beatles, especial Paul who, with his feminine appearance and thin eyebrows, looked gay. The group decided to play a trick on Bernie and didn't tell him what kind of club they were in. Berine pointed out a girl he fancied and one of the group would lie to him and say he had slept with her. Bernie started to chat up the girls and The Beatles left him to it. Later, he re-joined the group and told them "I've just had a wank off this great-looking bird in the lav." The lads still didn't tell him the truth but he soon found out for himself. When they saw him the next day Bernie told them, "I put my hand down there and she's got a fuckin' knob".

Years later, after Pete Best was sacked from The Beatles, he returned to Hamburg with Lee Curtis and The All Stars in March 1963. According to Joe Flannery, the group's manager, Pete was unknowingly dating a transvestite for a week. The local girl was a regular at the Star-Club where Lee Curtis and The All Stars were playing and her good looks attracted the group's drummer. Pete started dating the girl until things got a little serious in the bedroom and Pete discovered her secret and quickly ended the relationship. It seems, despite Pete's experience with The Beatles, the transvestites of the Reeperbahn could still trick a man into bed.

But back to the story of The Beatles. The group were now living above the club in the attic on the fourth-floor. They shared two army bunk beds between the four of them. Stuart, still an active member of the group, was living with Astrid. It wasn't the nicest of places but the conditions were still much better than the Bambi-Kino and The Beatles would often take girls back to the attic regardless of how many other Beatles were already in the room. John, who slept below Paul, once wrote in a letter to Cyn complaining that he couldn't think over the noise of Paul and his girlfriend on the bunk above.

One night, the boys took a girl up to their room and the four of them took it in turns to make love to her. Later, excited, they told Horst "We've all just screwed the same bird". Sometimes the group would walk in on one and another having sex and Paul remembers a time when he walked in on John with a girl. "That was the intimacy we had" he recalls. According to Paul there was two kinds of girls that would visit the Top Ten, "The Reeperbahn girls"-the barmaids, the strippers, and the prostitutes, and "a nicer class of girl" who came to the Reeperbahn at the weekend. Most of these girls were under eighteen and had to leave by ten o'clock but not to worry, there was always time for a quickie in the toilets before the clock struck ten.

In April, Cyn and Dot arrived in Hamburg and the party was over. With both their boyfriends being in the same band, Cyn and Dot became good friends and in the Easter holidays they set off to Hamburg together. When the girls arrived at the train station in Hamburg they were tired and hungry,they had been travelling for two days and couldn't wait to see their boyfriends. When they got off the train however they couldn't see John or Paul anywhere.

After a while they noticed John and Paul running towards them. The boys were exhausted, reeked of alcohol, and their clothes hadn't been washed for a week. They had been up all night, playing in the club until two and then staying awake the rest of the night high on pills. The boys took them to the Seaman's Mission for some much needed breakfast but afterwards they went their separate ways. Cyn was to stay with Astrid while Dot would stay on a house-boat belonging to the toilet attendant at the Top Ten Club. John and Paul went back to the Top Ten for some much needed sleep.

John and Paul spent all their spare time with Cyn and Dot during their two week stay. They showed them around the city including the Reeperbahn and the girls in the windows. Every night Astrid, Cyn, and Dot would go to the Top Ten club to watch the band play. They too started taking preludin so they could stay up with the boys. During the breaks in the band's performance, John and Cyn would sneak off to the men's toilets for a quickie before John was due back on stage. Some nights John would beg Cyn to stay with him the night in the flat above the club and the couple would share John's bottom bunk. The boys bought their girlfriends new clothes, leather skirts, and jackets, and in John's case, a pair of leather knickers. Paul bought Dot and himself gold engagement rings like the ones Stuart and Astrid had bought each other a few weeks previous. When John saw the rings he said to Cyn "Perhaps we should get engaged too" but, thinking it was far too soon, Cyn turned him down. The girls returned to England in the middle of April allowing the boys to return to enjoying Hamburg's seedy nightlife.

Another performer at the Top Ten club was twenty-year-old Tony Sheridan from Norfolk. He had started his career in Hamburg in 1960 playing at the Kaiserkeller before moving on to the Top Ten. The Beatles would often back him on stage and one night in May 1961 a German singer called Tommy Kent walked in to the Top Ten club and watched Tony Sheridan being backed by The Beatles. He was impressed. The next day, he told his producer, Bert Kaempfert, about what he had seen and Bert agreed to go with Tommy to the Top Ten the following night. Tommy spoke to Paul and asked if he could play with the band on stage. They played four numbers including 'Be-Bop-A-Lula' and 'Kansas City'. After, Tommy introduced Paul to Bert who told him he would like to record Tony Sheridan and The Beatles. The group and Tony both agreed and the next day they signed a contract with Bert and Polydor. The recording sessions took place on 22 and 23 June in Friedrich-Ebert-Halle in the south of Hamburg. The Beatles recorded six songs with Tony Sheridan and two on their own. One, 'Ain't She Sweet', features John Lennon on lead vocals. When the songs were released, The Beatles had had their name changed to The Beat Brothers. Bert thought 'The Beatles' sounded too much like 'The Peedles' which was a German slang word for a small penis. Had The Beatles become popular in Hamburg because they were little pricks? It's an interesting theory.

The only group members that didn't appear on those recordings was Stuart. Stuart was spending more and more time with Astrid and less time with The Beatles. It wouldn't be long before Stuart would leave the band all together, handing over the part of bass player to Paul.

On 2 July, The Beatles left Hamburg but they would return again in April 1962. This time they were playing at the biggest club in the area-The Star-Club. The Star-Club was owned by thirty-four-year-old Manfred Weissleder. Manfred had moved to the St. Pauli area in the 1950s and began working at the Tabu bar. He soon began producing his own films and after the success of his 3D erotic films he opened a sex club on Paradiehof which backed on to a cinema and restaurant called Stern-Kino on Grosse Freiheit. Manfred owned an erotic movie theatre in the same building and soon took over the entire building and it became the Star-Club.

When The Beatles arrived in Hamburg tragic news was awaiting them. Their friend and former band member, Stuart Sutcliffe, had died three days before. He had died suddenly of 'cerebral paralysis due to bleeding into the right ventricle of the brain'. He was only 21. When Astrid meet the group at the airport she was alone. "Where's Stu?" they asked expecting their friend to be there and Astrid broke the sad news. On hearing the news of his best friend's tragic death John broke down in floods of tears which quickly turned into hysterical laughter.

The Beatles kept going and so did the drinking, drug taking, and the sex. The group was now living in an apartment across from the club. One day Pete packed up his gear and left. He was moving in with his stripper girlfriend. Now it was just Paul, John, and George sharing the one room. One day John walked in on Paul in bed with a girl. Unlike when Paul had walked in on John and then walked out again, John decided to play a trick on the girl and cut her clothes to shreds. One of the girls John was taking back to the apartment was Bettina Derlin, a blonde barmaid who worked at the Star-Club.

Bettina, better known as Betty, had photographs of her favourite Liverpool bands hanging on the wall of the bar where she worked. Several of the photos were of John and on one of them she had written 'Prelly King'. (Prelly was a nickname for preludin) In-between sets The Beatles would gather at the bar and put their chins on the counter. Betty would lean forward and push her large breasts in their faces. John started to date Betty and the pair would go to the cinema together to see horror films. John liked to watch Dracula starring Christopher Lee but Betty didn't like horror films and would cover her eyes and ask John to tell her when the gore was over. John would wait for the worst bit and shout "Now!"

It wasn't long before Betty became pregnant with John's child. When he found out he insisted she had an illegal abortion. Illegal abortions were often dangerous and Betty ended up with a glandular condition. John and Betty would meet up again in 1964 and again in 1966 when The Beatles returned to Hamburg to play a concert at the Merck Halle. Backstage, the group meet up with some of their German friends including Bert Kaempfert, Astrid Kirchherr and a woman named Cattia who had been one of Paul's Hamburg girlfriends. Another of Paul's girlfriends was Ruth Lallemannd. Ruth, like Betty, was a barmaid at the Star-Club but it wasn't just barmaids that became the group's girlfriends.

One night John picked a girl out of the audience who he fancied. While the group played, the girl caught John's eye and during a break he approached her. She was a large girl called Margo and Tony Dangerfield, an English musician working in Hamburg at the time, remembers "John used to go round with a big fat chick called Margo". Margo would go everywhere with John but only for a short time of course, there was too many girls in Hamburg for any full time relationships and the Star-Club had all the best looking ones. The club charged 50 pfennigs entrance fee but the pretty girls got in for free. Many of the girls were strippers or prostitutes-not that The Beatles ever had to pay for their services. Girls that wanted to sleep with the band members would stand near the stage in an area called Ritzenecke (Ritz Corner), known as

'Cunt Corner' by the bands that played at the Star-Club. An average of 20-25 women would stand there every night. The Beatles were like four boys in a candy store but better still, everything was free.

John's letters home to Cyn continued and in one dated April 1962 he tells her he wishes he was on his way to her flat with the Sunday papers, chocolates, and 'a throbber'. He clearly missed Cyn but was he behaving himself? He ends the letter with 'ooh it's a naughty old Hamburg we're living in!!' Paul too was writing letters home but he was also writing songs. Two songs that he wrote in Hamburg, 'Love of The Loved' and 'P.S I Love You' were written for his Liverpool girlfriend, Dot.

But Paul couldn't just stick to one girl and another of Paul's Hamburg girlfriends was Erika Hubers. Erika was a pretty nineteen-year-old girl with long hair. Her father owned a club on Grosse Freiheit, the street where The Beatles were playing and Erika herself was a waitress in another club in the area. One night she saw The Beatles playing at the Star-Club and took a liking to Paul. The two started dating in April 1962 and Erika became pregnant. At the end of May The Beatles returned to Liverpool and it was around that time that Erika realised she was with child. When The Beatles returned to Hamburg in November, Erika informed Paul she was pregnant and Paul insisted she had an abortion but at eight months pregnant it was far too late. The Beatles left Hamburg again two weeks later and returned for the last time in December 1962. On the last day of their visit, 31 December, Erika gave birth to a baby girl who she named Bettina. Legal action was taken by Erika's father and papers were filed. When the legal papers arrived on the desk of David Jacobs, Paul's attorney, he advised Paul to remain silent and the complaint was never answered. Years went by and in 1966 Erika's father threatened to file legal papers again, this time in London where the whole case would be made public. Worried about his public image, Paul paid Erika £13,000 to keep quiet. The secret was kept quiet until 1981, when Bettina sued Paul for the sum of three million pounds. In 1983, Bettna posed nude for High Society magazine and was paid £600. She claimed she did it because of delays in maintenance payments from Paul. That same year Paul underwent two separate blood tests which came back negative proving he was not the father. However, in 2007 Bettina claimed that Paul had used a double to take the blood test and the signature on the documents he signed were also fake.

4

Beatle Babies

Back in Liverpool, The Beatles were making a name for themselves playing in various clubs in and around the city. Still dressed in the leather trousers and jackets they had worn in Hamburg, The Beatles were like no other group on Merseyside. They were much rawer, they played straight rock 'n' roll while the other groups wore suits and were imitating The Shadows. Night after night, hordes of girls would turn up at the clubs to see The Beatles play, sometimes queuing for hours before the club opened. Bob Wooler, the DJ at the Cavern, began playing 'My Bonnie', The Beatles' German single with Tony Sheridan, every night. Fans started going in to the local record store, NEMS, and asking for copies of the single. The manager of the store, Brian Epstein, began to take interest in the group and found out they played regular lunchtime session at the Cavern club, just up the road from NEMS.

One afternoon Brian took a trip up to the Cavern and liked what he saw. In December 1961, he invited the group to a meeting in his office at NEMS where he proposed the idea of managing the group. On 24 January 1962, The Beatles signed a five-year contract with Brian.

Brian Epstein was born to Jewish parents, Malka (later known as Queenie) and Harry Epstein, on 19 September 1934. He had a younger brother, Clive, born in 1936. His father, Harry, owned North End Music Stores (NEMS) in Liverpool. Brian worked at the store in its record department and the store soon became one of the biggest musical retail outlets in the North of England. When a second store was opened on Whitechapel, Brian was put in charge. Things were going well for Brian but he had a dark secret-Brian Epstein was a homosexual. Homosexuality was illegal in Britain at the time but Brian's love life was somewhat of an open secret in Liverpool. Everyone knew but nobody spoke about it. At sixteen, Brian had wanted to be a dress designer but when his father opposed the idea he started working in his father's store. In December 1952, he was drafted into the Royal Army Service Crops as a data entry clerk. He was posted to the Albany Street Barracks near Regent's Park in London. Brian had a string of gay lovers while in the army. These were mainly men he would pick up in public toilets while dressed in an officer's uniform. He was spotted hanging around the public toilets, chatting up men and after ten months he was discharged on medical grounds and returned to Liverpool and the family business. Brian had always had an interest in the theatre and in 1956 he decided he wanted to join the Royal Academy of Dramatic Arts (RADA) and in September he passed the audition to study at RADA in London. Again, Brian was seen hanging around public toilets picking up men and in 1957 he left the course and again return to the family business in Liverpool.

One night, in February 1956, Brian met a man in the Lisbon Pub in Liverpool. Brian began talking to the muscular man who he learnt was working on the docks. The man told Brian that he liked him and Brian liked him too. At closing time Brian offered the man a lift and they ended up driving through Sefton Park. The two began making love in Brian's car and once they had finished the man demanded Brian's wallet, threatening to kill him if he refused. The man then hit Brian twice in the face, knocking him out. While Brian laid unconscious on the ground, the man stole his car keys and drove off in his car. Brian turned up to Joe Flanney's house covered in blood. Joe, also a homosexual, had been friends with Brian since the two had been children and it was Joe that Brian had turned to when he first discovered his own sexuality.

Brian had been spending a lot of time at the Playhouse Theatre and had visited the pubs and bars in the area which, although strictly not gay bars, were popular with the homosexual community of Liverpool. It was during these visits that Brian came to realise that not only was he attracted to the company and the lifestyle of the men that frequented the bars but he was attracted to the men themselves. Not able to tell his family, Brian turned to his closest friend, Joe Flanney, and told him that not only was he homosexual but he liked "rougher boys". Now Brian had been attacked by one of those rougher boys and had turned to Joe once again. Joe took care of him and cleaned him up and let him stay the night but the trauma wasn't over. The man had contacted the Epstein family demanding money to keep the story secret. The Epsteins contacted the police and the police arrange for Brian to pay the man the blackmail money, the man was arrested and sent to prison. During the court case Brian was referred to as 'Mr.X'.

Sex in 1950s Britain was something that happened between a married man and his wife and even then it was thought of as being a marriage duty performed by the woman to pleasure her man. Women gained no pleasure from anything that happened beneath the sheets in 1950s Britain-there was no such thing as the female orgasm and husbands had no idea about the G-spot let alone where it was located. Sex before marriage was frowned upon by sociality and was a sin according to the church. It wasn't unusual for young adults to still be virgins on their wedding day. Not only that, but sex was somewhat of a mystery to the unmarried. There was no sex education and a lot of young people were confused about sex before their wedding night. Talking about sex was highly taboo and the act of love making was surrounded by rumours and myths. One such myth was that a woman could become pregnant from sharing a toilet seat with a person of the opposite sex. Another myth was that masturbation would lead to blindness.

Homosexuality had no place in 1950s Britain, not only was it illegal but it was not openly accepted by the general public. Homosexuals were thought to be the way they were because they were 'perverts'. Being gay was a risky business especially in Liverpool and other cities with a tough macho image. There was no safe way to pick up men even in the bars and pubs that were known for their gay clientele. Chatting up the wrong man could lead you into some serious trouble, you could be attacked and beaten, you risked being arrested and a prison sentence, you risked losing your job or, like Brian Epstein, you risked being blackmailed.

Another risk for homosexual men was being sent to a mental asylum. Homosexuality was seen by many as a mental illness that could be cured. It was common for young men, sometimes with pressure from their families, to voluntarily commit to spending time in Rainhill Mental Hospital in Merseyside to be rid of their homosexual inclinations. Part of the treatment involved the patient being shown heterosexual pornography in an attempt to stimulate his dormant heterosexuality. They would then be given drug aversion therapy while being shown homosexual pornography. Of course, none of this had any effort. This kind of treatment, along with the shame and ridicule and the other risks mentioned above were well known by Brian and were the reason his sexuality, like that of other homosexual men in

Liverpool, (including Joe Flannery-later a music manager and Cavern Club DJ, Bob Wooler) had to be kept a secret.

After the Mr. X case, which made the papers, rumours began to spread that Brian was Mr.X. Brian dealt with the rumours by dating a couple of woman. If he could be seen around town with a woman on his arm his secret would be safe. The first was Sonia Seligson who Brian took to the theatre, dinner-dances, ballet, and classical concerts. One night, drunk, he proposed to her but she ignored him. The couple never slept together and Brian would spend weekends in Paris in the company of men. Once Sonia found out about Brian's secret life she ended the relationship. Brian's second and last girlfriend was Rita Harris. Rita was a NEMs employee who started dating Brian around Christmas 1959. They never slept together and Brian admitted to being gay. The pair remained friends.

Despite the constant fear of being outed as a homosexual, there were times when Brian could relax and enjoy the company of other gay men in what would now be considered as Liverpool's gay scene. Brian, along with his friend Joe Flannery, spent a lot of time at the Playhouse Theatre and the bars and pubs surrounding it and Queen's Square including The Magic Clock, The Royal Bar, and The Stork Hotel. The usual clientele, although not all of whom were homosexual, including actors, academics, solicitors, barristers, businessmen, and artists but also included the odd thug or blackmailer looking to make a quick buck from an unfortunate man who happened to choice the wrong man to chat up.

Brian liked masculine men and no doubt when he first set eyes on The Beatles, in their leather gear rocking the Cavern, part of the attraction was sexual. Brian felt the same way about The Beatles as most of their female fans. The music was good, and played a major role, but, at the end of the day, he just wanted to fuck them or at least touch them. It's no surprise then that when Brian watched The Beatles perform live at the height of their career he joined the girls at the back and screamed his head off.

Shortly after signing the group, Brian made a move on Pete. One bank holiday Brian, Pete, John, and Cyn drove to Blackpool in Brian's car. The four of them stopped off for a pint and Brian asked Pete if he would like to spend the night with him in a hotel. Pete politely refused saying, "Er not my cup of tea, sir." Brian didn't approach Pete again and the two of them never spoke about it. Back in Liverpool, Brian didn't have to invite men back to hotel rooms. In 1961, he rented a flat at 36 Falkner Street. He had no intentions to ever live there, he didn't even fully furnish the apartment and was still living at home. His one and only use for the flat was for his sexual liaisons. Brian could take men back to his flat and his family would be none the wiser.

Brian wasn't simply in the music business to get closer to the men he fancied, although there was a few including Pete Best, Tommy Quickly, Lee Curtis, John Lennon, and Michael Haslam. The music business of the late 50s and early 60s was one of the few occupation were a man could be openly gay (the others being the theatre-which Brian had already tried and hairdressing). Being gay and in the music business was far from unusual, in fact, it was fairly common. By 1963, Brian had already made friends with composer Lionel Bart, musician Russ Conway, and producer Joe Meek, who were all gay men working in the music business and who had all spent time in Brian's company in Liverpool.

Other gay band managers from that era include Larry Parnes-who managed a stable of young male stars including Tommy Steele, Billy Fury, Marty Wilde, and Vince Eager. Simon Napier-Bell-who managed The Yardbirds and John's Children, whose guitarist was Marc Bolan, who letter went on to lead T.Rex and have an affair with his manager, Napier-Bell. Kit Lambert was also gay and managed The Who, whose lead singer, Pete Townshend was bisexual and nursed a crush on Mick Jagger.

Sex and attitudes towards sex changed massively during the 1960s. Poet Philip Larkin wrote in his poem Annus Mirabilis :

>   Sexual intercourse began
>   In nineteen sixty-three
>   (Which was rather late for me)

Between the end of the Chatterley ban
And The Beatles' first LP.

'The Chatterley ban' is a reference to the 1928 novel Lady Chatterley's Lover by DH Lawrence which had been banned in Britain until 1960. The following year the contraceptive pill was introduced as a prescription drug for married women only. The Pill wouldn't become widely available until 1974 but by the end of the sixties, however, the number of users had rose from 50 thousand to one million. Sex became much more of a pleasure for both men and women regardless of their marital status. Sex out of wedlock increased massively during the 1960s and despite abortion being illegal in the UK until 1967, backstreet abortions were common and 35,000 women a year were treated by the NHS for botched abortion attempts while another 10,000 women a year had terminations at West End clinics, like the one in Harley Street, for large sums of money. 1967 not only saw the legislation of abortion but Leo Abse's Sexual Offences Act legalised gay sex between men in England and Wales. (It would be some time before it was legal in Scotland (1981) and Northern Ireland (1982)).

As The Beatles became more popular, the crowds of girls became larger. When they played afternoon sessions at the Cavern girls would skip school and travel from all over Liverpool to queue up outside to get in and see the band play. The queue would stretch down Matthew Street but always at the front was a group of girls John called 'the

Beatlettes'. The Beatles and the Beatlettes built up a special relastionship, the Beatlettes would stand at the front of the stage, bringing the band drinks and shouting out song requests. The Beatles were always kind to the Beatlettes, bringing them tea and soup while they queued outside the Cavern. Sometimes they would even give them free tickets.

The fans adored the group but they took a disliking to the group's girlfriends. Whenever Cyn would go to the Cavern to see the group play she would get called a 'slag' and would often hear the fans talking about her. "What's he doing with her?" they would ask each other. Other times, jealous fans would threaten to beat her up. John wasn't even the most popular of the group, Pete, their drummer, was. Pete was considered the best looking of the group and when the girls screamed they screamed for Pete. He was known as "mean, moody and magnificent" and due to his popularity, Pete was given his own singing spot during the group's act. Paul would take over drums and Pete would move to the front of the stage where he would perform 'Peppermint Twist' by Joey Dee and the Starliters. While singing he would do the twist on stage and occasionally a girl from the audience would be invited on stage to dance with him. One night a girl called Kathy Johnson got up on stage to dance with Pete. Seeing that Pete was enjoying himself, the band played for longer so the two could dance more. The pair enjoyed themselves so much that they started going out and in 1963 they got married.

The group could escape the teenage fans at a pub across the street from the Cavern called the Grapes. The Cavern didn't have a licence to serve alcohol so the Grapes was the perfect venue for bands to drink before and after gigs at the Cavern. The Beatles' regular seats were located across from the ladies toilets and for good reason too. In the evenings, before The Beatles played at the Cavern, young women would arrive at the Grapes direct from work in their headscarves, hair rollers, and work clothes. The women would constantly be in and out of the toilets, getting changed, doing their hair and makeup. The door was almost always open and the group could see the workers in various stages of undress. The boys, especially John, would often wolf whistle and shout out crude remarks and on some occasions the lads would get a cheeky flash.

As The Beatles' fanbase grew they began to need a road manager to get them to and from gigs across Merseyside. Their first roadie was Frank Garner, a bouncer at the Casbah club. Not able to do both jobs, Frank had to quit and in February 1961 Pete asked Neil Aspinall to drive them back and forth. Eighteen-year-old Neil had been lodging with the Best family since 1960 and was helping Mona Best run the Casbah. In July 1962, Neil left his job as an accountant and began working for The Beatles fulltime. Mona, then thirty-six, had recently separated from her husband, John, and was now having an affair with Neil. In October 1961, she became pregnant and a baby boy was born in late July 1962. He was named Vincent Roag Best and to avoid controversy his father was registered as being John Best. John Best hadn't been near Mona for months and the whole of Liverpool knew Neil was Roag's real father. In August 1962, Pete was sacked from The Beatles and was replaced by Ringo Starr. Neil decided to continue working for the group and ended his relationship with Mona, leaving her and their three-week-old son.

Ringo Starr was born Richard Starkey at 9 Madryn Street in Liverpool on 7 July 1940. He was the only child of Elsie and Richard Starkey. His parents divorced in 1943 and Elsie remarried. Her second husband was a painter and decorator called Harry Graves. During his childhood, Ringo was in and out of hospital with various illnesses. In 1955, he worked as a delivery boy for British Rail for a few months. He then worked as a barman on a ferry travelling back and forth from Liverpool and New Brighton. Ringo would use his job to chat up girls. "I'm in the navy" he would tell them. He wasn't of course but it seemed to work because it was around this time that he lost his virginity at the age of sixteen.

Ringo and a friend had visited a fairground held at Sefton Park where they managed to pull two stunning girls. The boys fancied their chances and took the girls to the grass at the back of the fairground where the four teens began making love while 'Ghost Riders in the Sky' played in the background. "It was really exciting" Ringo would remember later.

Ringo's first real girlfriend was fourteen-year-old school girl Patricia Davies. Patricia, better known as Pat, was three years younger than Ringo and was best friends with Pricilla White (later known as Cilla Black). Pat and Cilla both wanted to became hairdressers and would go round to Ringo's house on Wednesday nights and practice on Ringo's mother, Elsie. The girls would bleach and cut Elsie's hair and she would cook them Spam and chips for tea.

In 1957, while working as a trainee joiner at Henry Hunt and Sons, Ringo and his friend Eddie Miles formed a skiffle group with three other employees. The group, the Eddie Clayton Skiffle Group, was taking up a lot of Ringo's time and he decided it would be best if he and Pat went their separate ways. Ringo's next group was another skiffle group, the Darktown Skiffle Group. It was at Litherland Town Hall while playing with the Darktown Skiffle Group in 1957 that Ringo first met his next girlfriend. Geraldine McGovern, better known as Gerry, was a factory girl who lived near Ringo. The two started dating in 1958 and in March 1959, Ringo joined his third band, Al Caldwell's Texans, who later became Rory Storm and the Hurricanes. Ringo spent a lot of time with Gerry, the two became very close and in 1960 they became engaged. Ringo's grandfather gave him his gold wedding ring for the wedding which was to take place the following year. Meanwhile, Rory Storm and the Hurricanes played a summer session at Butlin's holiday camp in Wales from July to September.

Butlin's was a haven for young men wanting to get their leg over. The holiday camp had a string of young girls coming and going each week. Those girls were looking for a good time and a holiday romance and who else better to have a week-long fling with than a member of the resident band, Rory Storm and The Hurricanes. During their stay at Butlin's none of the band went to bed alone. The number of girls in the band's chalet would even result in the band being kicked off the site in the summer of 1961. It wasn't always easy pickings for the band however and Ringo remembers one night when the band travelled to London to play a gig and found none of the girls were interested in the scouse boys. At the Lyceum the group lined up and one by one they asked the same girl to dance. "Piss off" was the reply they got. Eventually, Ringo managed to get a dance from a French girl "who didn't know any better."

In October, they went to Hamburg were they played at the Kaiserkeller club, topping the bill above The Beatles. Like The Beatles, Rory Storm and the Hurricanes had their fair share of sex in Hamburg-Butlin's had nothing on the Reeperbahn. One of Ringo's Hamburg girlfriends was Heike Evert. Heike, better known as Goldie, remembers

Ringo taking her to the cinema, sometimes with Paul tagging along.

By March 1961, everything was in place for Ringo and Gerry's big day. Wedding cars had been booked and the reception hall was reserved but there was one problem. Gerry wanted Ringo to put her first. She didn't think being a musician would get him very far and wanted him to get "a proper job" before she would marry him. Ringo remembers "it was her or the drums" and he choice the drums. Gerry gave back her ring which Ringo gave to his mother who wore it until the day she died. Ringo continued to play with Rory Storm and the Hurricanes until August 1962 when he joined The Beatles.

By 1962, three of the four Beatles (John, Paul, and Ringo) had steady girlfriends. Ringo was now dating sixteen-year-old Maureen Cox, a petite brunette known to her friends as Mo. Maureen was a regular fan at the Cavern Club. She first saw Ringo playing with Rory Storm and the Hurricanes when she was fifteen. At one point she dated Johnny 'Guitar' Byrne, the rhythm guitarist of Rory Storm and the Hurricanes. She once kissed Paul for a bet but it was Ringo who her heart was set on. One afternoon, after The Beatles finished their set at the Cavern, Maureen got Ringo's autograph and kissed him. Weeks passed before Ringo even noticed Maureen and he later admitted having no recollection of the meeting as a lot of fans were doing the same thing at the time. It wasn't until the end of 1962 that Ringo first took note of Maureen.

Ringo bought his first car, a hand painted red and white Standard Vanguard, when he was 18. After playing with Rory Storm and the Hurricanes at Butlin's he was able to afford a better car, a blue and cream Ford Zodiac. "I was The King in that car" Ringo remembered later. Owning a car was extremely important for young men wanting to impress the ladies. It was equally as important as being on stage, which is why cars have often been the subject of rock 'n' roll songs. From 'Rocket 88' to 'Maybellene', rock 'n' roll has always been about fast cars and loud guitars and here was Ringo, a drummer in Liverpool's best band, with a very fancy looking car. Ringo was in fact the first Beatle to own a car with Paul McCartney following suit purchasing a Ford Consul Classic in 1962 while George owned a Ford Anglia. Already being married, John Lennon didn't have much use for a car of his own and was the last of the four to pass his test. When he final passed his test in 1965 he bought a Ferrari. The back seat of a car was a perfect place to enjoy some quality time with a lady friend. Paul wrote the song 'Back Seat of My Car' in 1969 shortly after hooking up with Linda Eastman and John went as far as having the back seat of his Rolls Royce converted into a double bed. Before that, Neil's van was ideal for a quickie with fans after gigs.

One afternoon when Ringo pulled up outside the Cavern Club in his Ford Zodiac he noticed Maureen among the crowd of girls. Ringo smiled at her and asked if she was going to the show the next night, she was. Ringo then asked her if she wanted to go out after the show but Maureen turned him down saying she had a curfew. Not put off, Ringo arranged a date for the afternoon instead.

Ringo picked her up from Ashley Du Pre's, the beauty salon where she worked, and the two spent the rest of the day together. They went to the park and then to see the singer Frank Ifield, then to the cinema for a double feature, then to the Pink Parrot for drinks before ending the night at the Blue Angel. From that night on Ringo and Maureen became an item.

Paul and Dot were still dating but had begun to see less and less of each other. When they did spend time together they would argue. Paul told Dot she could no longer visit the Cavern to see the band play. Thinking it would help The Beatles career if the fans didn't know the band had girlfriends she agreed. Dot soon realised the real reason was that Paul was seeing other girls and wanted to keep them a secret from her. In July 1962, Paul turned up at Dot's flat and told her they had been going out for so long they could either get married or end it. Then Paul told her he didn't want to get married and ended the relationship there and then.

One of the girls Paul had been dating on the sly while still with Dot was Iris Caldwell, George's ex-girlfriend. Iris, now seventeen, was working as a dancer. In December 1961, she got a job performing at the Tower Ballroom in New Brighton. On Boxing Day, The Beatles were performing at the Tower Ballroom and that night Iris and Paul met for the first time. Paul couldn't take his eyes off Iris as she danced to 'The Twist' and by the end of the night he had asked her out on a date. The couple went on dates to the cinema every Tuesday and in July 1962, when Paul broke up with Dot, he made Iris his official girlfriend. Just as Paul had cheated on Dot with Iris he would cheat on Iris with one of John's ex-girlfriends, Thelma Pickles.

Thelma had remembered Paul from her time dating John but found now he had developed from a little plump schoolboy into "someone very much his own person." Thelma hadn't kept up-to-date with The Beatles success and was shocked when the pair went on a date to a coffee bar and a girl asked for Paul's autograph. She was even more shocked when she went to see the band play at the Cavern and found girls screaming for her boyfriend. Like Cyn, Thelma found that when The Beatles' fans found out she was dating Paul they treated her very unfairly. They would follow her after the show and shout names at her. Thelma didn't last long and Paul went back to only seeing Iris and the two became more serious.

Paul and the other Beatles would spend a lot of time at the Caldwell's family home at 54 Broad Green Road. The house was named Stormsville after Iris' older brother Rory Storm and The Beatles even gave names to Iris' parents. Her father, Ernie, was given the name The Crusher while her mother, Violet, was called Violent Vi. Stormsville became a late-night hang-out for the local teenagers. The Beatles and their friends would go there, drink tea, play cards and chat. One night, The Beatles, Iris, Cilla Black, and her friend Pat (Ringo's ex) used an Ouija board to try and contact their dead relatives. Seeing Paul and Iris together made George jealous and he wanted his old girlfriend back. Whenever the two had a row George would phone Iris and ask her if he could take her out. Paul and Iris eventually ended the relationship when Paul met and fell in love with Jane Asher.

Another favourite hangout for Merseybeat bands in the early sixties was Joe Flannery's home at Gardner Road. The Beatles started to spend time at Gardner Road in 1962 when Pete was still a member of the group. The house was behind the recently opened Granada Bowling Alley on Green Lane and The Beatles and other groups would spend a lot of time playing ten pin bowling. Back at Joe's house The Beatles would enjoy tea and toast prepared by Joe's Norwegian house keeper, Anne. Anne would take care of The Beatles and the other groups, cooking for them and cleaning and ironing their clothes. John would sit in an armchair by the fire and scribble endless doodles on scraps of paper before falling asleep for the night. In the morning, Anne would throw the drawings into the fire. Anne's daughter Girda was a stunning but shy girl who became popular with many of the musicians that would spend time at Gardner Road. Out of The Beatles, it was Paul who had a crush on Girda but she was so shy she would run and hide in the kitchen if he as much as looked at her.

As The Beatles began to take off, Brian banned any girlfriends from hanging around with the group. The fans had already shown their jealously and Brian didn't want The Beatles to lose any fans because of it. Iris and Paul, however, could spend time together at Stormsville after the group had played at the Cavern. By the time The Beatles went to Hamburg for the last time in December 1962 they had already had a top twenty hit with 'Love Me Do'. Paul and Iris' relationship had to be kept secret and when Paul wrote letters to Iris he would have to sign them 'Paul McCoombie'. Despite the rumours, 'Love Me Do' was not written about Iris. The song had been written before the two met. Another song, 'I Saw Her Standing There', about a seventeen-year-old dancer, was in fact about Iris.

Iris was always suspicious that she wasn't the only woman in Paul's life and she wasn't wrong. Paul was never the kind of man to stick to just one woman and while dating Iris he was also dating a girl called Celia Mortimer. He started dating the seventeen-year-old art student and Beatle fan in March 1962 after he broke up with Thelma Pickles. Celia, an attractive redhead, made her own clothes and was into Trad Jazz before seeing The Beatles play. "Paul was attractive, intelligent, arty, all the things that appealed to me" she said later. The couple would sit in Celia's dad's front room and her friend's front room, holding hands and kissing. They would go to the cinema together and in October they saw the first James Bond film, Dr.No. Later that month they hitchhiked to London to visit Paul's old friend Ivan Vaughan who was now working as a doorman in Soho. Ivan's flat only had one bed and that night Paul and Celia had to sleep on the floor.

One of George's girlfriend around that time was Ann Marie Guirron. Marie, as she was known, had been dating George since mid-June 1962. She was a slim, attractive blonde eighteen-year-old who worked in the Cotton Exchange and knew Jim McCartney. "I fell for George the first time I saw The Beatles" she recalls. The couple started dating and "I was soon head over heels for him" she remembers. George would pick her up in his Ford Angella and take her out to eat or bowling after gigs. On his days off, they would go to the cinema or on long drives, sometimes ending up in Wales. They would visit each other's homes where they could make love. Other times they would make love in George's car. Marie would later date Justin Hayward of The Moody Blues and the pair married in 1969.

George's next girlfriend was a seventeen-year-old blonde fan called Benadette Ferrell. Benadette worked in the salon above NEMs on Great Charlotte Street. She had been on one date with Paul but it was George she liked and they began dating in

October 1962. He would pick her up from work and take her to the cinema. As far as the fans were concerned The Beatles were single and free to date and sleep with them. The Beatles had grown accustomed to quickies or 'knee-tremblers' in dark alley ways or shop doorways after a gig. It wasn't uncommon for the fans to become pregnant with a Beatle baby.

Alistair Taylor, Brian Epstein's assistant, remembers the first time such a thing happened. He was working at NEMS when he was approached by a couple and their teenage daughter. They wanted to speak with Brian but he wasn't available so, Alister told them he would pass on the message. The girl, Jennifer, was around seventeen and was five months pregnant with John's child. They told Alister that Jennifer would be keeping the baby and wanted John to pay towards its upkeep. Alister took notes and when Brian rang later that day he told him the story. "Do you believe them?" Brian asked. He did and a few days later Brian arranged for the family to meet with him in person. Brian paid Jennifer £250 and agreed to pay a weekly maintenance for the child until it was 16 under the condition that the baby's father would be kept a secret. Even John wasn't told. Jennifer was only the first of many girls that were paid by Brian to keep their Beatle babies quiet. Alister would even hand out a few cheques himself. There could have be up to 400 babies born to Beatle dads in Liverpool.

Perhaps the most bizarre Beatle baby claims came

about in 2011, when Brittany Starr, a contestant on the American talent contest TV show So You Think You Can Dance, claimed to be the daughter of Ringo Starr. Not only that but she claimed that after the death of John Lennon in 1980, her father, Ringo Starr, went into hiding in Utah where he married a 25-year-old woman called Cynthia. She also claims that Ringo was then replaced with a look-a-like who signed a contract to give him the rights to name Ringo Starr while the 'real Ringo' started his new life. If true, the whole history of The Beatles would have to be rewritten. The story received little attention from the local media and the 'real Ringo', a toothless old man dressed in a pink Sgt. Pepper's suit, was interviewed. Not only did the old man not look like Ringo but he spoke with an American accent. The 'real Ringo' also seems to lack 'fake' Ringo's money and locals have reported that he is never seen out of his Sgt. Pepper's outfit. Locals have also claimed that he wonders around Salt Lake City talking to himself. Since the story broke the 'real Ringo' has met with fans and given out autographs, something the 'fake' Ringo no longer does. The biggest problem with this story is that Brittany was born in August 1980, which doesn't fit in with her story which has the 'real Ringo' moving to Utah in December 1980. During conversations with the author in 2013, Brittany changed her story several times saying that the contract signed by the real and fake Ringo was signed between 1968 and 1973, her parents had met sometime between 1976 and 1978 and she was born in 1984, which in no way adds up with the story told in 2011 nor could Brittany proved the author with any evidence of the supposed contract, her parents' marriage or her birth.

In the first months of 1962, John met a girl called Lindy Ness. The two would write long letters to each other and some still survive today. It is unknown whether Lindy and John were lovers or just friends but she was definitely more than just a fan. John would sometimes reply to fan mail, especial in the early days, but he would always sign those letters 'Love from John Lennon' with two or three kisses. In his letters to Lindy he would sign 'Love from John' with a lot more kisses. One letter came with as much as twelve kisses. The length of John's letters to Lindy also suggest that she wasn't just a fan. John's replies to fans were always short while his letters to Lindy would take up pages. John opened up to Lindy in his letters and in one, dating from December 1962, John talks about how Hamburg was no longer fun. "I'm so cheesed off I could bloody cry." he writes. He also talks about Lindy being at the airport, presumably when The Beatles left for Hamburg on 18 December. The letter finishes with John saying he'll be home next Sunday and would see Lindy in a week. The Beatles returned to England on 1 January 1963. It's clear that Lindy Ness was more than a fan, was she a friend? Was she more? Who Lindy Ness was is a mystery, until now. Linda Ness was a fourteen-year-old beatnik and a member of the campaign for Nuclear Disarmament when she first saw The Beatles playing at the Cavern in December 1961. "John Lennon in a leather suit was a sight to behold" she remembers. She loved The Beatles and with her friend, Lou Steen, she began bunking off school to visit the Cavern at lunchtime. Sometimes the two girls would be given lifts home in Neil's van at the end of gigs. Lou Steen remembers "Nothing sexual happened, not even a kiss". The girls were just fourteen and the lads knew their limits. "We never realistically thought we had a chance of shagging one of them" Lou recalls. Linda became close to John and he gave her the nickname Lindy. They were photographed together outside the Cavern and on 8 April 1962 she visited Mendips to meet Mimi and have tea with John and his cousin David Birch. They talked, ate cake, drank tea and watched TV. "His Aunt is weird" Lindy wrote in her diary that night. By now, Lindy was 15 and John was seeing a lot more of her. They would spend hours talking and sometimes Lindy and her friend Lou would stay over at Paul's house with John and John would brag that she was his "Jail Bait". "People assumed we were having a sexual relationship" Lindy remembers. If only she had been a year older things might have been a little different. By the time she had come of age it was 1963 and The Beatles had moved on and so had Lindy Ness.

John loved Cyn and wanted to be with her but he couldn't keep it in his pants and in 1961 he started dating Beatle fan Patricia Inder. Pat, as she was known, had first met John and the other Beatles in 1958, when she was fifteen and John was eighteen. Pat became friends with the group and they began hanging out together. She remembers "John had a great sense of humour and a big personality." Pat would take the group to her friend Sue's flat where they would eat chips, smoke cigarettes, drink cheap wine, and listen to rock 'n' roll records. The group would scribble down the lyrics to the songs on scraps of paper so they could learn them. At first, Pat wasn't interested in John and instead had a crush on Paul. With her long blonde hair and slim figure, Pat was right up John's street and in 1961 the two friends became lovers. "Until then, I hadn't really been attracted to John" Pat remembered in 2009 "But you know what they say-It's in the kiss." After playing at the Riverboat Shuffle aboard a River Mersey ferry, the MV Royal Iris, in August John invited Pat to a party at Sue's flat.

When the couple arrived at the flat however it became apparent it was a party for two and John admitted he had arranged for the two to be alone. Pat lost her virginity that night and in 2009 she told The Daily Mail "He said he'd be gentle with me, which I realise sounds corny." Afterwards, the couple laid together wrapped in each other's arms. John told Pat she had beautiful eyes and kissed her eyelids. Despite Pat knowing about Cyn, the couple continued their affair for over a year. Pat would sit at the Cavern and watch The Beatles play while Cyn was left at home. On one occasion, when Cyn did go to the Cavern, John told Pat to wait for him after the show. Minutes after he had kissed Cyn goodbye and watched the taxi drive off he was in Pat's arms. Pat wasn't happy about the situation and told John she felt she was wasting her time but John told her one woman was never enough for any man. He loved Cyn but he told Pat he was in love with her too.

Pat remembers that John would always keep his socks on in bed and always had his guitar with him. Often after making love he would sit up in bed and strum away. Despite having two girls on the go at once, John couldn't help feeling insecure and would ask Pat if she thought he was ugly and if she thought The Beatles were going to make it. One night after a gig John took Pat to a restaurant and the two became tipsy after drinking a couple of bottles of wine. In a narrow alleyway on the way home John suddenly turned to Pat and said "Marry me Pat!" Thinking he was joking she told him to stop messing around and nothing else was said of the matter.

Meanwhile, in August 1962, John's girlfriend, Cyn, found herself pregnant with John's child. When Cyn told John he didn't response. A few minutes passed before he said "There's only one thing for it, Cyn. We'll have to get married." And that's exactly what the couple did. On 23 August John and Cyn got married at the Mount Pleasant Register Office in Liverpool. (The same place John's parents had married.) The wedding was to be a small affair,

Brian wanted the marriage to be kept a secret. He feared if the fans found out it would be the end of The Beatles. Ringo, who had only just joined the group, wasn't even told. The wedding was attended by George, Brian, Cyn's brother Tony, his wife Marjorie and Paul who was best man. John's aunt, Mimi, and Cyn's mother, Lillian, didn't approve and neither of them attended the wedding. After the wedding, Brian Epstein bought everyone dinner at Reece's. That night John was away with The Beatles playing at the Riverpark Ballroom in Chester.

It wasn't until December that Pat found out that John was married and Cyn was pregnant. John had kept it a secret but, just before The Beatles went to Hamburg, Paul took Pat to one side and filled her in. She confronted John who told her they could continue the affair but Pat ended the relationship and didn't see John again until 1965 when she met him backstage for a few minutes at Hammersmith Odeon.

As a wedding gift, Brian Epstein let John and Cyn live in his flat at 36 Falkner Street for free. For John and Cyn this was the first time the two could live together and not worry about being disturbed by anyone else. It was at the flat that John wrote 'Do You Want to Know a Secret' about his and Cyn's secret marriage. When Cyn went into labour, on 8 April 1963, John was away playing with The Beatles. She gave birth to a baby boy who was named John Charles Julian Lennon. Three days would pass before John would visit Cyn and their new born son on 10 April. Like the marriage, the child, known as Julian, had to be kept a secret and John turned up to the hospital in a disguise. Twenty days after the birth of his son John would go on a holiday with The Beatles' manager, Brian Epstein.

Before John and Brian's holiday, Brian took a weekend trip to Hamburg with Joe Flannery in the summer of 1962. Brian and Joe had both heard stories of the night life and the sexual freedom of the Reeperbahn and Brian wanted to experience it for himself. During their weekend in Hamburg Brian was able to experience a couple of young men who were able to satiate his secret desires. For one weekend, Brian could relax and be himself. Hamburg could offer things that Brian and Joe couldn't even dream of back in Liverpool and now they were free to experiment with their strangest fantasies.

5

Spanish Love Affair

Throughout 1962, Brian and John became very close and by March 1963, John was a frequent guest at Brian's London parties. Peter Brown, a friend of Brian's who would later become his assistant and director of NEMS Enterprises, recalls how the two were very rarely apart. John was by Brian's side when he opened the NEMS office in London, Brian introduced John to the gay scene of the West End theatre crowd and John would attend Brian's parties. London's gay scene was alien to John and he was fascinated by it. Peter Brown remembers how John would stand in the corner trying to look as tough as possible. John's macho look only attracted the men even more. In 1980, John would tell one reporter "Brian was in love with me. It's irrelevant."

In April, Brian asked John to go on holiday with him to Barcelona. In the last week of April the British press announced that all four Beatles would be taking a holiday in the Canary Islands. Three of The Beatles did fly out to Tenerife on 28 April. John and Brian however took a separate plane to Barcelona. In 1970, John recalled how he left his wife and newly born son, Julian, to go on holiday with Brian. "Cyn was having a baby and the holiday was planned, but I wasn't going to break the holiday for a baby: I just thought what a bastard I was and went". The pair would sit in cafes in Torremolinos and watch men as they passed by. John would point out a man passing and ask Brian if he liked him or not. Brian would point out what he found attractive or unattractive about the man. John was enjoying himself "I was rather enjoying the experience, thinking like a writer all the time: 'I am experiencing this'" he said in 1980. John watched on as Brian picked up men. "I watched Brian picking up boys" he said in 1970 "And I liked playing it a bit faggy-It's enjoyable."

Rumours spread across Liverpool like wildfire. Were John and Brian having a secret love affair? The rumours continue to this day. What, if anything at all, happened between John and Brian during that holiday is still to this day shrouded in mystery. John would always deny anything sexual happened between the two. "It was almost a love affair" he would later say "but not quite. It was never consummated." Or at least that was what he said in public. According to his old school friend, Pete Shotton, John one night told him that Brian had come on to him one night. John dropped his trousers and told him "Stick it up me fucking arse then". Brian told him that's not what he wanted and instead John let Brian "toss me off". When John had finished this tale Pete remarked "What's a wank between friends".

Allen Klein, who managed The Beatles after Brian's

death, remembered John telling him a different story. He told Allen that he had tossed off Brian. Peter Brown, however has yet a third story. He remembers how Brian told him that he had given John a blowjob. A friend of Brian's, Simon Napier-Bell, who received a long answer machine message from Brian the night he died, claims that Brian revelled to him that he and John had slept together at least twice. A lot of people who were close to John and Brian discard the rumours as nonsense. Paul McCartney has gone on record several times claiming that John had agreed to the holiday with Brian to assert his leadership of The Beatles. This is nonsense of course, Brian Epstein was fully aware that John was the leader of the group, John had made this clear since Brian first met The Beatles in 1961.

In June, Paul held a party for his 21st birthday. The party was held at his Aunt Jin's house on Dinas Lane in Liverpool, where a marquee was erected in the back garden. Guests included The Beatles, Billy J. Kramer, The Shadows and the Cavern Clubs DJ Bob Wooler with Liverpool band The Fourmost provided the entertainment. During the party Bob Wooler joked with John about the rumours about him and Brian. "Tell us John, how was the honeymoon?" the DJ asked. A very drunk John responded by hitting him in the nose. He then grabbed a nearby shovel and hit him in the head with it. Bob fell to the floor and John continued to beat him with the shovel. Suddenly, John realised if he hit Bob once more he could kill him. He restrained himself and three men seized him and disarmed him. Bob was left with a broken nose, a black eye, a cracked collarbone and severely bruised ribs. Brian took Bob to the hospital. John then turned on a girl called Rose, groping her breasts. Rose reacted by slapping John across the face then, according to Billy Hatton of The Fourmost, John punched her in the face, knocking her to the ground. Billy J. Kramer, witnessing the events from across the garden, shouted "Lay off, John!" John called her a little slapper and then turned on Billy saying "You're nothing, Kramer. We're the top!" Billy Hatton, who was closer, intervened and came between John and Rose before he started to put the boot in. John's friend, Pete Shotton, was at the toilet while all this was going on and when he returned he found John sitting on the floor with his head in his hands, moaning "What have I do?" When John saw Pete he asked if the two could swap wives for the night. The answer was a strong no and John went home with his own wife that night. Cyn took him home muttering "he called me a fuckin' queer". The national press got hold of the story and the Daily Mail ran it on their back page. John had to issue a telegram apologising to Bob and Brian had to pay a £200 settlement. Had John become so angry because something had happened in Spain? "I must have been frightened of the fag in me to get so angry" John would say later.

After the party, John's attitude towards Brian changed. He would often make cruel remarks to Brian which would sometimes reduce him to tears. John would make fun of the fact that Brian was Jewish and homosexual. When Brian wrote his autobiography, A Cellarful of Noise, in 1964 John offered Brian some alternative titles that included 'A Queer Jew' and 'A Cellarful of Boys'. When John's cruel jibes became too much Brian would turn up at Joe Flannery's house where he could pour his heart out.

In April, The Beatles were rehearsing at the Royal Albert Hall in London. Seventeen-year-old actress Jane Asher was writing a piece on the group for the Radio Times. Jane was already a well-known actress by the time she met The Beatles and had appeared on Juke Box Jury. Watching her on a black and white television set the group thought she was blonde but when they met her in real life they found out she was in fact a redhead but still attractive.

After the rehearsal, Jane took The Beatles to journalists Chris Hutchins' apartment to interview them. Chris opened a bottle of Mateus Rose and toasted The Beatles. As they drank wine, Jane interviewed the group. As the interview drew to a close and John became drunk things took a turn for the worse and the end of the interview couldn't be published at the time for obvious reasons:

John: Yeah, the group the fans love so much they want to tear us to pieces.

Jane: Oh, John. You're such a cynic. Admit it, you adore the attention.

John: Sure I'm a cynic. What we play is rock 'n' roll under a new name. Rock music is war, hostility and conquest. We sing about love, but we mean sex, and the fans know it.

Chris: The fans think you're decent, clean-living chaps.

John: It's just an image, and it's the wrong one. Look at the Rolling Stones. Rough as guts. We did that first and now they've pinched it.

Ringo: You can't blame them for that.

Jane: The fans have a dream that one day they might marry a Beatle.

John: Yeah, but only those who haven't reached the age of puberty. I give some girl an autograph and she wants my tie or some hair. Then she wants to have sex. Then she tells me she's only 15. Jailbait. Is there any more booze?

Chris: That's the last of it. I wasn't expecting company.

John: OK, there's no booze. Let's talk about sex. Jane, how do girls play with themselves?

Jane: I'm not going to talk about that!

John: You're the only girl here and I want to know.

How do you jerk off?

Chris: There's only one jerk here.

John: Oh fab! No booze, no birds, insults from the host....what kind of rave is this? Bleedin' marvellous. I'm going in search of some crumpet. Call me a taxi.

Jane: You know, John, you can be very cruel sometimes.

John: It's the beast in me.

John then left, leaving Jane crying and being comforted by George. At the end of the night George took Jane home with him but it wouldn't be long before Jane started dating Paul. Paul and Jane's relationship became public when they were photographed together leaving the Prince of Wales Theatre after a date to see the play Never Too Late.

John narrowly avoid another national scandal in 1963. Even though he was married he began dating seventeen-year-old Ida Holly. Ida was a DJ who worked at the Majestic Ballroom in Liverpool. It was there that she met John. John's marriage to Cyn was a secret and Ida was unaware of it when she first started dating John, who was five years her senior. After their first date John tried to undress Ida. He unzipped her dress "down to the bum", Ida spun round and slapped him across the face. John was impressed. Ida wasn't like most of the teenage fans he was used to and the couple saw each other for about six months. Ida was with John in February 1963 when The Beatles reached number one for the first time with their second single, 'Please Please Me'. Ida was a few minutes late meeting John that day at the Walker Art Gallery. When she arrived, John rushed through the revolving doors shouting "We're number one! We're number one!" He lifted Ida into the air and swung her in his arms. The two then headed to Brian's office at NEMS to join the celebrations. Celebrations which John's wife, Cyn, had not been invited to. John and Ida continued to see each other right into the summer of 1963. One day, Ida's father found out about John's marriage and threatened to expose John to the press. Ida confronted John who told her marriage was only a piece of paper. Ida was not happy and ended the relationship there and then. She also convinced her father not to go to the press.

Ida Holly wasn't the only seventeen-year-old fan dating a Beatle. In 1963, Bernadette Farrell was dating George. She had been a fan of the group since 1961 and was a regular fan at the Cavern Club. When 'Love Me Do' was released Bernadette bought a copy which George later signed. When The Beatles got their first silver disc for 'Please Please Me' George brought it to Bernadette's house to show her and Bernadette's mother asked if she could play it on the record player. While George was away at the Canary Islands with Paul and Ringo, Bernadette was photographed by

Merseybeat for their Face of Beauty series. When George got back to Liverpool, Bernadette was waiting for him. She had done her make-up and put her hair in rollers. When George turned up looking "very bronzed and beautiful" he took one look at Bernadette and said, "So this is the face of beauty". Benadette jumped up and ran upstairs "with a brush in my hair before you could blink." As The Beatles became more popular and the group spent more time away from Liverpool, Bernadette and George decided to break up.

While dating Maureen, Ringo did not stay faithful. He was also dating another girl called Paula Bennett. Paula was part of a group made up of four girls that would follow The Beatles around Merseyside and attend their every gig. The other girls were Pat Davies (Ringo's Ex) Louise Steel and Linda Robinson. The girls remember Paul being very kind and the only one who would dance with them in-between sets. It was Paul who arranged for the four girls to travel with the group in the van so they could get to and from the gigs. It was Ringo, however, not Paul, who Paula liked best. She remembers he was "wonderful fun to be with". The two started dating in 1963 and they would hang around at the Blue Angel together. As The Beatles became famous, Ringo became worried a journalist would snap a photo of the two. This would affect the group's popularity but that wasn't the main problem. Ringo didn't want Maureen to find out about him and Paula and he started seeing less of her.

In August 1963, John and Cyn finally got to go on their honeymoon after being married for a whole year. John planned a week for the couple in Paris and Julian was packed off to stay with John's aunt Harrie. The couple stayed at the George V hotel and for the first couple of days they spent time alone, seeing the sights of Paris and spending many hours in the hotel room making love. A couple of days into their stay, they received a message from Astrid. She was in Paris for a couple of days and wondered if they wanted to meet up. John and Cyn met up with Astrid and one of her friends in a wine bar in Paris. The four of them knocked back glass after glass of red wine, moving from one bar to the next. They ended up at Astrid's lodgings where, after more wine, the four of them got into bed together. This may have not been how Cyn had pictured her honeymoon but for John it was perfect.

When The Beatles moved to London in the summer of 1963 they first lived in the Hotel President in Bloomsbury. In October they all moved into a flat at 57 Green Street-John left his wife and son behind in Liverpool. The Beatles became friends with The Rolling Stones and The Moody Blues. They would often visit The Moody Blues at their flat in Gunterstone Road. Living in the same building was Angie King, who would later marry Eric Burdon of The Animals. Angie shared a flat with Cathy Etchingham who would become one of Jimi Hendrix's girlfriends and a girl called Ronnie who later married Zoot Money. Billie Davis lived next door with Brian Jones of The Rolling Stones. The Beatles started to hang around in clubs like Speakeasy and Bag O'Nails. There they could pick up girls and take them back to the flat at Gunterstone Road.

Tony Bramwell, a friend of The Beatles who worked for NEMS, remembers that The Beatles and their friends, including Tony, had more than their fair share of London girls. "Sometimes, we'd find ourselves in bed with two girls at a time" he wrote in his book 'Magical Mystery Tours, My Life With The Beatles'. The Beatles and their friends would travel up to Golders Green to meet girls from Ada Foster School for Drama. The girls there were known for being easy and the lads renamed the school Ada Foster School for Dirty Little Slappers. Six of the girls lived together in a flat on Fulham Road and The Beatles and their friends would be regular visitors to the flat. When they arrived they would tell the girls "Don't bother to get up". They had come for one thing and one thing only. The girls wanted to be famous and were willing to fuck their way to the top.

Shortly after The Beatles moved to London so did one of Ringo's girlfriends, Paula Bennett. Paula had moved to London to study sociology at London University. Ringo had pretty much ended his relationship with Paula back in Liverpool but now she was in London things were different. He continued to date Paula even though he was still seeing Maureen back in Liverpool. The couple started going on dates to the Ad Lib Club and at the end of the night Ringo would pull his coat collar up over his face to avoid being recognised by the press. Again, Ringo was protecting himself as much as he was protecting the group's image.

Paul wasn't so lucky when it came to avoiding negative press. In July 1964, the press got hold of a story that could have shattered The Beatles careers. Seventeen-year-old Anita Cochrane claimed Paul was the father to her new born son, Philip. Anita had been fifteen when she first met Paul in 1962. She was heading to the Cavern on Matthew Street and Paul and John were coming the other way. A mutual friend introduced them and Anita remembers "I immediately fell for him." Paul asked her if she could go to the Tower Ballroom in New Brighton the coming Friday. Anita agreed and she got ready for her first date with her first boyfriend on her sixteenth birthday. Dressed in a grey gymslip dress with a black polo-neck jumper and black tights, Anita headed to the Tower Ballroom where she watched The Beatles play. After the gig, Paul took her to a cafe in Liverpool called Joe's. They drank coffee and chatted for hours then Paul asked her if she wanted to go to a party. Anita agreed to go but the party turned out to be a bedsit with two friends. The couple went to bed but Anita was nervous. She told Paul she was still a virgin but he reassured her and made her feel more relaxed. As the pair made love Anita kept her clothes on as much as possible. Looking back Anita recalls "I was too shy to take them off". Anita thought that night was to be the beginning of something beautiful. She really liked Paul. "I thought he was a knight in shining armour" she remembers but, for Paul, Anita was just another easy lay. When he dropped her off at the bus stop the next day he didn't arrange to see her again. When she got home she rushed to her room and cried her eyes out.

Anita became a regular visitor to the Cavern in the hope that Paul would talk to her or at least notice her. Paul began to notice Anita in the crowd and he would give her a quick smile or dedicate a song to her. Anita struck up a friendship with John and he would invite her to the parties he held at his flat on Gambier Terrace. Some nights Anita and Paul would end up together, kissing and cuddling. One night at John's flat the couple slept together again. Paul treated Anita exactly the same way he had the last time they slept together but Anita wasn't put off. For sixteen months Anita didn't date anyone else. She only wanted Paul but Paul saw her as nothing more than a little play thing he could pick up and put down whenever he wanted. One night in April 1963, when Anita and her friend Gill were walking home, Paul drove past and picked the girls up. He took the girls to John's flat and that night Gill slept with John while Anita slept with Paul for the third and last time.

Shortly after that night Paul and Anita were together at a friend's flat. Paul was joking about how easy Anita was, Anita got up and threw her cup of coffee over him, Paul slapped her and called her a slag, Anita left and ran all the way home in tears. She began seeing other men and Anita's friend, Gill, remembers Anita dated Mike Hart from a band called The Road Runners for a while. She had a one-night stand with a man too and it was around this time that she realised she was pregnant. Anita worked out she had conceived around the end of April, the same time she had slept with Paul for the last time. Anita wrote to Paul telling him she was pregnant with his child but she got no reply. Anita's next move was to visit Paul's father, Jim. Jim was very kind and invited Anita and her mother in. The three of them chatted over cups of tea but then Jim broke the bad news. "Paul says he doesn't know you. That's all I can tell you." he told Anita. Anita left feeling very upset and betrayed. She knew the truth, everyone at the Cavern knew the truth but Paul was denying everything.

Having an out of wedlock child was deeply scandalous in the early sixties. Everything had to be kept a secret. Anita would have to move in to a mother-and-baby home and when the child was born he would be given up for adoption. On 10 February 1964, at Billinge Hospital near Wigan, Anita gave birth to a baby boy who she named Philip Paul Cochrane. When Anita set eyes on the baby she fell in love and decided to keep him. Anita contacted Paul again but all her letters and telegrams were ignored. In March 1964, Anita and her family visited lawyers in Liverpool to try and get financial support from Paul. The Cochrane's lawyer, D.H Green, contacted The Beatles chief solicitor David Jacobs and Anita was first offered £2 10s a week until Philip was 21. Anita turned down the offer and was made another offer of £5 a week maintenance. Paul was still denying that he was the father and D.H Green decided Paul should appear in court and have a blood test.

No doubt the media would find out and so, wanting to avoid any negative publicity, Anita was offered a one-off payment of £5,000 which she accepted. Like Jennifer before her, Anita had to sign a contract saying she wouldn't say who the child's father was. The contract didn't apply to Anita's friends and family who already knew the secret. When The Beatles returned to Liverpool for the Northern Premiere of their film A Hard Day's Night on 10 July 1964, notices began to appear in telephone boxes and fliers began to circulate accusing Paul of being a "cad" for not supporting his son. Lengthy poems about the child were circulated to the newspapers. They read in part:

> My name is Philip Paul Cochrane, I'm just a little boy...
> In spite of all her lovin' we got no thanks from him
> It seems he loved my mother, just long enough to sin
> Besides his lust, she took his money to compensate a lie
> But Mr. Paul McCartney, Dad, you make mother cry.

Nothing much came of it and the story was never published. Everyone in Liverpool already knew about Anita and Paul.

Philip had known who his father was from an early age and had been shown the contract his mother signed when he was eight. Philip didn't want anything to do with his father and even though he was in a band himself he preferred reggae to the songs of The Beatles and Wings. In 1983, when Peter Brown published his book 'The Love You Make: An Insider's Story Of The Beatles', he told the story of Anita and Paul. The press soon tracked down Anita and Philip and Anita started getting hate mail. The pressure of the press drove Philip into drugs and he began stealing to feed his heroin habit. Philip joined a rehabilitation centre in West London where he remained for two and a half years. In the mid-1990s, Philip moved to London to start a new life. Things were just getting back on track when, in 1997, a relative sold the story to a Sunday newspaper for a five figure sum. When the story broke both Anita and Paul issued statements denying that Paul was Philip's father. In May 1997, Anita gave an interview to the Daily Mail telling her story. In the interview she admitted that Paul may not be Philip's father but it was very likely that he was. She asked Paul to take a DNA test but he refused. In 2001, Philip tracked down the man Anita had had a one-night stand with. The man had a DNA test which proved positive, proving that Paul was not the father. It should be noted that in Peter

Brown's book, 'The Love You Make: An Insider's Story Of The Beatles', Anita's name is changed to Alice Doyle.

Anita wasn't the only woman to claim she had had a child fathered by Paul. In 1993, a 33-year-old American woman claimed to be Paul's daughter. Michelle Le Vallier, who had changed her name to Michelle McCartney, claimed Paul met her French mother, Monique, in London in 1958, when Paul was only sixteen. The two had an affair and a child was born in Paris on 5 April 1959. Monique had died in 1992 and had never claimed to have ever met Paul. Michelle later produced a birth certificate that stated James Paul McCartney as her father. Paul was asked to take a DNA test but again he refused. The birth certificate was proven to be fake and the whole story was dismissed as nonsense with Paul's publicist Geoff Baker saying "This woman is no more Paul's daughter than I am".

6

Polythene Pam

By 1964, The Beatles had toured the UK four times and had made a trip to Sweden. During one of those tours, in August 1963, John would experience something that would later influence him to write the song 'Polythene Pam'. On 8 August, The Beatles played two concerts at the Auditorium in Guernsey. After the concert, John met up with his friend Royston Ellis. Royston was a beat poet that John called "England's answer to Allen Ginsberg". A year younger than John, Royston first met the Beatles in 1960 when he came to Liverpool to read poetry at the university. Royston was bisexual and when he first saw George Harrison at the Jacaranda he fancied him. "He looked fabulous" Royston said years later. He started talking to him and George told him about The Beatles. Royston arranged for the group to back him while he read poetry at the Jacaranda. One of his poems, Julian, had lines in it the sounded like they were about gay sex. Paul remembers thinking it was about "fucking sailors". Royston even spent a few nights with John at his flat on Gambier Terrace where he spoke about the Soho night life and told the group that one in four men were 'queer' although they might not know it. "We looked at each other and wondered which one it was" Paul remembered later. He was now working as a ferry boat engineer in Guernsey and had heard The Beatles were in town. When John met up with Royston and his girlfriend, Stephanie, they took him back to the attic flat Royston was renting. The three discussed poetry and John told Royston he had always liked one of the lines in one of his poems: I long to have sex between black leather sheets and ride shivering monocycles between your thighs. Royston suggested they should try it out but without any leather sheets at hand they made do with oilskins and polythene bags. The three of them dressed in polythene bags and got in bed together. Royston and John then took turns to make love to Stephanie. When later asked if he had had a sexual experiences with John, Royston replied, "Yes, but there was a girl between us". Stephanie wasn't the only girl to influence the song 'Polythene Pam'. Another girl from Liverpool called Pat Hudgett also had a role to play. Pat had first seen The Beatles play in 1961 when she was fourteen. She attended their gigs regularly and was one of the girls the group would give a lift to in their van. By 1963, she was sixteen and working as a barmaid in Liverpool. One night after a gig she slept with John. Pat had a habit of eating polythene and had been given the nickname Polythene Pat. "I just used to eat polythene all the time" she recalls "I'd tie it in knots and then eat it. Sometimes I even used to burn it and then eat it when it got cold."

The tour then took the group to Jersey and Blackpool before moving on to Wales where they played six nights at the Odeon Cinema in Llandudno. During their stay in Wales the group was visited by two old friends, Liverpudlian musician, Kingsize Taylor and John's old German girlfriend, Bettina Derlin. Bettina had talked Kingsize Taylor into taking her back to England with him so that she could be reunited with her long lost lover. When they arrived at the hotel The Beatles were staying in they were told that the boys were rehearsing at the Odeon so, Kingsize Taylor and Bettina waited for them. On his return, John took one look at Bettina and kept on walking. He didn't even say hello. He sat at the other side of the lobby where he switched on his transistor radio. Only Ringo spoke to Kingsize Taylor and Bettina. Heartbroken, Bettina returned to Hamburg where she was last seen by Kingsize Taylor working in the red light district. She would get a second chance at meeting up with John again in 1966 when The Beatles played in Hamburg. This time John was a lot friendlier and even posed for photos with his ex-girlfriend.

One night in November, after a date with Jane, Paul missed the last train back to Liverpool and ended up staying the night at the Asher's family home. At the time Paul was living in a flat in Green Street with Ringo and George but he didn't like it there and so he moved into the top floor of the Asher's family home. The top floor had two bedrooms and a bathroom which Paul shared with Jane's brother, Peter. At night, Paul would sneak into Jane's bedroom on the floor below so that the couple could make love. Paul and Jane were often seen in public going on dates to musicals, classical concerts, plays, and exhibitions. The couple went on a holiday to Greece in September 1963, with Ringo and his girlfriend, Maureen. By January 1964, Paul and Jane had become so serious that Mersey Beat had to run a report denying rumours that they were planning to marry. Brian Epstein was quoted as saying "Paul is definitely not engaged or married". This was to be the first of many rumours and stories about the couple as the press absolutely loved the pair.

Jane Asher was born in London on 5 April 1946. Her father, Richard, was an eminent physician and her mother, Margaret, was a music teacher who had taught George Martin to play the oboe. Her sister, Clare, was a radio actress and her older brother, Peter, was born 22 June 1944 and later formed the duo Peter and Gordon, who had hits with the McCartney penned songs: 'A World Without Love', 'Nobody I Know', 'I Don't Want To See You Again', and 'Woman'. Peter was later employed by The Beatles' record company Apple.

The female fans in Liverpool had been jealous of the band's girlfriends and in John's case, his wife. They had called them names and threatened them. One fan had even hit Ringo's girlfriend, Maureen, in the face. The fans in London were very different. When Cyn moved to London in 1964, the young family moved into a flat at 13 Emperor's Gate. The flat was on the sixth floor of the building and there was no lift. Cyn had to climb up the six flights of stairs carrying Julian, a pram and whatever shopping she had. Beatle fans soon discovered the address and would gather outside both day and night. If the front door was left open they would get inside, sleeping in the hallway with sleeping-bags and Thermos flasks. When Cyn took Julian out in his pram fans would surround them. The pram would almost disappear as it was swarmed by fans wanting to look at the baby or hold him. The fans loved Cyn almost as much as they loved John. They would ask her where she got her hair done or where she got her clothes from and they would tell her she was lucky to have John. Cyn tried her best to be nice to the fans but sometimes felt intimidated and frightened by them. She needed to get away and so, when The Beatles went to America for the first time in February 1964, John took Cyn with him. She was the only woman on the trip.

Brian was still very keen on The Beatles keeping their relationships a secret. John, on the other hand, was having none of it. One night before they flew to America he told Cyn he wasn't going to keep her a secret anymore. Although no announcement was made, the fans and the press in Britain soon found out about John's wife. The secret first became public knowledge in July 1963, when Melody Maker reported that John was married and wondered if being married would affect pop stars. When asked about it John's reply was "no comment". When The Beatles left Britain on 7 February 1964, the press got their first photo of John and Cyn together at Heathrow airport just before they boarded the plane to America. It wasn't until the group returned from America on 22 February that John was first asked about Cyn. "Did your wife enjoy it over there?" the reporter asked. "She loved it" John replied before jokingly asking "Who? Who?" "Don't tell them he's married" adds Ringo "It's a secret".

John's secret was out, Brian's, however, wasn't. In England, Brian lived in fear of the press getting a hold of the fact that he was gay. Not only could it end his and The Beatles' careers but he could be sent to prison. Record producer Joe Meek had been convicted of "importuning for immoral purposes" in 1963 and was fined £15. The story made the papers and consequently, Joe became the subject of blackmail. Brian was worried something similar might happen to him. In September 1964, Brian's nightmare came true when he got wind that a slur campaign against him had begun in Liverpool. His sexuality had been outed in his home town and rumour had it that the music paper Mersey Beat was going to make his sexuality public. Worried, Brian took action the only way he knew how and purchased the newspaper outright from Ray McFall and immediately fired Virginia Harry, who he believed had something to do with the slur campaign.

Brian never once had a long-term relationship, it

was too much of a risk to take. Liverpool had it's secret gay bars and pubs but, once The Beatles had made it, Brian had to stop visiting such places. Brian and Peter Brown were part of a little group of professional gay men that would visit each other's houses but they would never go out as a group. Brian and Peter would often drive to Cheshire, Wirral or Manchester together to go to a restaurant, pub or hotel. In London, Brian could enjoy the gay clubs in Soho but he had to be careful. In America however he was less known, he could relax more and enjoy himself.

Brian first went to America with another of his artist, Billy J. Kramer, who he had a crush on. Once in New York, Brian met up with his old Liverpool friend Geoffrey Ellis and composer Lionel Bart. Geoffrey and Lionel couldn't wait to introduce Brian to the gay scene in America. Brian absolutely fell in love with what the American gay scene had to offer. Geoffrey remembers "He behaved, sometimes, in a way which was very dangerous, and he was conscious of this. In some ways he sought out danger. It gave him a thrill." When The Beatles came to America, Brian took them to the gay bars and clubs. Paul remembers that at first the group wouldn't realise where Brian had taken them. "We were quite naive" he recalls.

The Beatles arrived in America on 7 February 1964, and the first people to visit them at the Plaza Hotel was the girl group The Ronettes. The two groups had first met a month ago when The Ronettes were on their first UK tour with The Rolling Stones. During that tour the girls (Sisters Ronnie and Estelle Bennett and their cousin Nedra Talley) had hooked up with members of the Stones. Ronnie was with Keith Richards while her sister, Estelle, was with Mick Jagger and Nedra was with Brian Jones. Ronnie would later remember the tour: "I remember times when the fog was so thick, we'd have to pull over. Keith and I would walk up to some stranger's house to ask for a cup of tea!" but she also remembers there was "not a lot of sex" between The Ronettes and The Rolling Stones.

During their trip to the UK, The Ronettes met up with The Beatles one night at a party. The girls had tried teaching the boys the latest teen dances, like the pony, the jerk and the nitty-gritty but Ringo was the only one who could get a hang of the moves. That night, George and Estelle paired off while John took a fancy to Ronnie. As the pair kissed, Ronnie expended to John that she was still a virgin and that she was saving herself for the group's record producer, Phil Spector. When The Beatles came to America, John didn't waste any time in trying it on with Ronnie again. John steered Ronnie off into one of the bedrooms, leaving his wife unpacking their bags. In the room Ronnie remembers "a handpicked audience was packed along the walls watching a young girl have sex every which way with one of the guys in The Beatles entourage". John quickly took Ronnie to another room where the pair started kissing. As he started to undo her dress Ronnie told John "I can't". Not impressed, John pushed her away, stormed out of the room, slamming the door behind him. The next day, he called up and apologised. Ronnie would eventually lose her virginity in June. She and Phil Spector had been listening to 'Do I Love You' for the first time when the couple made love. He'd promised her marriage but it would be another four years before they tied the knot.

John would have more success with Jackie DeShannon. The American singer was one of the support acts on tour with The Beatles in February 1964. She became close to John and the couple began an affair right under Cyn's nose. Years later, Jackie would call John her "soul mate".

While in America, Paul meet British actress Jill Haworth. The eighteen-year-old had recently split up with her boyfriend Sal Mineo. Sal Mineo and Jill had been dating for three years. Jill had lost her virginity to the actor at the Gotham Hotel in Manhattan when she was just fifteen. The couple broke up when Jill walked in on Sal, six years her senior, in bed with another man, Bobby Sherman. Jill first met The Beatles at a press conference at the Plaza Hotel in New York and afterwards invited Paul back to her apartment where the couple made love. When The Beatles flew out to Miami, Paul rang Jill and arranged for her to fly there. He even went as far as paying for the flight and hotel room but insisted Jill stayed at a separate hotel to the group.

Paul didn't want word of his affair getting back to Jane in England. Paul arranged for a car to pick up Jill from her hotel and bring her to the Beauville so the two could lock themselves away in Paul's room and make love for hours on end.

Back in England, John and Paul were dating sisters, Sandra and Alma Cogan. The Beatles first met Alma Cogan when they both appeared on Sunday Night At The London Palladium in January 1964. After the show, Alma invited the group back to the flat she shared with her mother and younger sister. The Cogan's flat in London had many famous visitors including Princess Margaret, Audrey Hepburn and The Beatles. The Beatles and Brian Epstein became regular guests at the Cogan's flat and were often joined by Lionel Blair. Alma, Brian and Lionel were all Jewish and became close friends. Brian would bring Alma presents from his trips aboard and once took her to Liverpool to meet his parents. Rumours began to spread that the two were romantically linked but, of course, Brian was gay and the rumours were untrue. Brian would help Alma in her music career, publishing her self-penned single 'I Knew Right Away'/'It's You' under his company, JAEP Publishing, which he had set up to publish George Harrison's songs. Paul helped out in the recording studio adding tambourine to the B-side.

John fancied Alma thinking she was really sexy. "John was potty about her" George later revealed. John started visiting the flat alone and he gave Alma the nickname 'Sara Sequin'. Despite John being married and Paul being in a serious relationship with Jane Asher, the two Beatles began dating Alma and her sister Sandra. Heavily disguised, John and Alma would book into hotel suites in the West End under the name Mr. and Mrs. Winston. Meanwhile, rumours spread about Alma's sexuality. Alma was unmarried and had never been seen in public with a boyfriend. Rumours spread across the showbiz world that Alma was a lesbian. Sandra says the rumours were untrue and that Alma had been involved with other men before and after John. Cyn became suspicious that her husband was having an affair "But I had no real grounds for suspicion" she remembers "just a strong gut feeling". John and Alma continued their affair until Alma died of stomach cancer in October 1966.

Keeping the affair a secret was not only important for John to protect his marriage but to protect his career. In Britain in 1964 everyone was aware how an affair could ruin the career of a person in the public eye. When John began his affair with Alma Cogan, in the first month of 1964, it had been just over six months since the media had found out about the now famous Profumo Affair. Conservative War Minister, John Profumo, had first met dancer and model Christine Keeler in 1961. Despite the 27 year age gap (Profumo was 46 while Keeler was just 19) and despite Profumo being married, the two began a sexual relationship. Unknown to Profumo at the time was that Keeler was also sleeping with drug dealer Johnny Edgecombe as well as Russian spy Yevgeni Ivanov. The affair lasted around a month but didn't become public knowledge until June 1963. Once it did, however, it became one of the biggest news stories of the year and wasn't out of the papers for months resulting in Profumo's resignation. If the papers had gotten hold of details of John Lennon's affair then it no doubt would have had a similar media coverage and could have resulted in the end of The Beatles' career or at least his marriage.

With Jane Asher busy with her acting career, Paul didn't have to be as careful as John. He could openly visit Sandra at the Cogan's flat. She remembers when Paul played 'Yesterday' to her on Alma's piano back when it was nothing but a tune. As he played the tune, Alma's mother, Fay, asked the couple if they would like some scrambled eggs. Suddenly, Paul began to sing 'Scrambled eggs, oh baby how I love your legs'. The song now had a title-'Scrambled Eggs'. Paul had first met Sandra in 1962, when she was a singer at The Establishment Club in Greek Street, London. The pair chatted after the show but they wouldn't see each other again until after The Beatles performance on Sunday Night at the London Palladium. Like John, Paul began to turn up to the Cogan's flat alone sometimes bringing presents for Sandra. A romance sparked up but it only lasted a few months. Paul was put off by Sandra's mother who was pushing for marriage. "I sensed the mum saying when I went to visit, 'That's a nice boy, darling, you could... you know?'" He later remembered "Looking back on it now, there was a sense of that."

In March 1964, The Beatles began filming their first film, A Hard Day's Night. Set to play a role in the film was seventeen-year-old English actress Hayley Mills. Hayley had previously been in Disney's Summer Magic, The Parent Trap, and Pollyanna. Hayley's character was to provide some romantic interest for one of The Beatles until the producer, Walter Shenson, changed his mind and Hayley's character was removed from the film completely. Hayley didn't completely lose out however as she was asked out on a date by George. George took her to a charity midnight premiere of Charade at the Regal in Henley-on-Thames. Hayley went on to appear in The Family Way in 1966. In the film she plays Jenny Fitton and in one scene see appears in the nude. Paul McCartney composed the film's soundtrack. George and Hayley didn't go on a second date as George now had his eye on another girl on the film set.

Eighteen-year-old model Pattie Boyd had been hired by Dick Lester to play the part of one of four schoolgirls on a train with The Beatles. Even though Pattie was a pupil from Ada Foster School for Drama she had never met The Beatles before and was star struck. She asked The Beatles for their autographs, George added seven kisses under his and then invited her back to his trailer. To George's surprise she turn him down. George wasn't put off and later that day he asked her out on a date. Again, she refused. Pattie had been dating thirty-year-old photographer Eric Swayne for two years. Still not put off George asked her out again the following Thursday and this time she accepted and ended her relationship with Eric. Within a week she had introduced George to her parents and a week later the relationship became public knowledge. George and Pattie took a holiday to Ireland where they stayed at the Dromoland Castle Hotel with John and Cyn. The hotel was besieged by the press who snapped photos of the couple and tried to get a comment from George. In the end the two Beatles and their women had to be smuggled out of the hotel in a laundry van. Rumours spread that the pair were engaged but when George was questioned about them he replied "She's my kind of girl and we like each other a lot, but marriage is not on our minds. It isn't a sin to have a girlfriend is it?"

From Brian Epstein's point of view, being in The Beatles and having a girlfriend was just that but by mid-1964 all four Beatles were in relationships and the whole world knew. There was nothing Brian could do about it, not that he needed too, The Beatles were now the biggest group in the world and the fans weren't going to be put off by Cyn, Jane, Pattie, and Mauureen and John, Paul, George, and Ringo weren't going to keep them a secret. They were even writing songs about their loved ones and in February, Paul wrote 'And I Love Her' for Jane. Paul wrote the majority of the song at the Asher's family home with John later helping him out with the middle eight. The group recorded it at the end of February and it was released on their third album A Hard Day's Night in June. The track was also released as in America as the B-side of 'If I Fell' in July.

In May, The Beatles and their women split into two groups and went on holiday. Paul, Jane, Ringo, and Maureen flew to St Thomas in the Virgin Islands on 2 May. Three days later George, Pattie, John, and Cyn flew to Waikiki in Hawaii, stopping over in Los Angeles. Once there, George was asked about Pattie; "She's my 29-year-old sister, my chaperone" he replied. On 4 June they kicked started their only world tour in Copenhagen. Ringo remained in London at the University College Hospital. He had collapsed during a photo session the day before with tonsillitis and pharyngitis and was temporary replaced by session musician Jimmie Nicol. The tour took the group to the Netherlands, Hong Kong, and Australia where Ringo re-joined the group. The group played six nights in New Zealand before returning to Australia to wrap the tour up.

For Jimmie Nicol, being a Beatle meant he now had sex on tap. "The day before I was a Beatle, not one girl would even look me over" he remembers. The day he joined The Beatles however all that changed, "they were dying just to get a touch of me". John Lennon took Jimmie under his wing and the two became friends. When the tour came to the

Netherlands, John was eager to show Jimmie the night life he could experience as a Beatle. Before playing a show in Blokker, the group flew to Amsterdam. There they were escorted by the police to the De Wallen Red Light District. John Lennon recalls "When we hit town, we hit it. There was no pissing about." Despite the police trying to avoid any kind of scandal, John remembers photos were taken of him "crawling about in Amsterdam on my knees coming out of whorehouses". Whatever happened to the photos is unknown but they have never been seen by the public. After spending hours in various brothels, the group made their way to the Femina night club. Jimmie Nicol was finding it hard to keep up. "I thought I could drink and lay women with the best of them" he said later "until I met up with these guys".

It was in Australia that John had his first sexual encounter with an Asian woman. Jenny Kee was a seventeen-year-old Australian girl with an Italian mother and Cantonese father. When The Beatles came to Sydney in June 1964, Jenny and her friend managed to sneak into the Sheraton Hotel in Kings Cross where The Beatles were staying. "We pressed all the buttons in the lift until it jammed" she remembers. The girls then made their way to the stairwell where they met The Beatles. "There was no holding back" she recalled year later. John spotter her, dressed in a tartan suit and black mod boots, and asked her if she's like to go to a party. "I wasn't a hardened groupie" Jenny remembers "I was very naive. I'd only had two boyfriends before that". John led her into his room and the two got into bed together. The first thing Jenny did was take out her contact lenses. "What are those?" John asked. The pair then made love "all night". "Sleeping with John Lennon was a fantastic thing" she later said. After, as the two laid in bed, Jenny heard screams and giggles coming from another Beatle and a girl in the next room. "He's with a Qantas hostess" John told her. Jenny would later move to London and one night she bumped into John at the Speakeasy club. John was with his wife Cyn but when he spotted Jenny he went up to her and whispered "contact lenses".

Jenny had sneaked into John Lennon's bedroom but she probably hadn't needed to. Mal Evans would pick girls that had been hanging around outside or in the hotel lobby and take them to a room where they would wait their turn to sleep with a Beatle. The girl's ages were never asked and more than once a member of the group came close to sleeping with an under aged girl. One girl in Adelaide even took home her blood-stained sheet as a souvenir after losing her virginity to one of The Beatles. Mothers, who had turned up to the hotel looking for their teenage daughters, would sometimes get so carried away with the idea of sleeping with a Beatle they would join the other women waiting their turn. And it didn't matter which Beatle they got and for The Beatles it didn't matter which woman they got as long as it wasn't one they had had before. Bob

Rogers, an Australian journalist who travelled with The Beatles throughout their world tour recalls "The boys never, to my knowledge, repeated the dose. They'd rather have a less attractive woman than the same one twice".

Jim Oram, another Australian journalist who travelled with the group on their tour remembers "A seemingly endless and inexhaustible stream of Australian girls passed through their beds: the very young, the very experienced, the beautiful and the plain". One of those girls was seventeen-year-old journalist Kerry Yates. Kerry was working for Woman's Weekly when she came to Sydney hoping for a story on Paul, who was celebrating his 22nd birthday. A large group of journalist and photographers crowded the hotel's corridor when Paul turned up to speak to them. Kerry had long blonde hair and was wearing a pink sweater that helped her stand out from all the grey and brown suits. Paul headed straight for her and invited her to his room. Kerry's photographer took photos of Paul surrounded by his presents and then was asked to leave. Paul told Kerry she could have an interview but first she would have to sleep with him. Knowing an exclusive story on Paul McCartney would help her career she was more than happy to agree. Years later she would never confirm or deny the claims saying "I'm not saying if I did it or if I didn't" but she got the story so we can only assume she did.

The group held a handful of parties in the hotel

room suites while in Australia. At one party a man had hidden a miniature Minox camera behind his tie and snapped photos of The Beatles as they drank and enjoyed their female company. It was Derek Taylor who spotted the camera and with the help of Tony Newman, the drummer with Sounds Incorporated, he managed to remove the film from the camera and eject the man from the party. What happened in The Beatles hotel room was to stay in The Beatles hotel room.

In August, the four Beatles flew to America for the second time. This time they left their partners back in England. The August trip to the states lasted a lot longer than their first trip in February which had only lasted two weeks. The group first touched down in San Francisco on 18 August and didn't return to England until 21 September. During the trip, rumours began to spread across the teen magazines that Ringo was romantically linked to actress Ann-Margret. The story first appeared in the magazine Confidential, who put the group on the cover of their August issue. The cover-lines read:

Psst! Who Hushed Up These Stories About The BEATLES?

* Their Wild Antics in a Hamburg Sex Cellar

* The Nite Two Beatles Went to Jail

* How Ringo Flipped for Ann-Margret

* The Marriage Nobody Talks About

*   Their Secret Love Life

The magazine claimed Ringo had "bent her shell-pink ears with an hour of long-distance oggly-googling, all in a special Teddy Boy lingo that left little Annie limp." Ann-Margret had previously been linked with Elvis Presley after co-starring with him in the film Viva Las Vegas. Ringo put the rumours to rest on 23 August when, in an interview with John, he told reporters that he had never even met Ann-Margret and denied ever ringing her or writing to her adding "I don't even write to my mother". The two Beatles also put to rest rumours about marriage, "I'm the only one who's married, folks" said John, and that John was expecting another baby with Ringo saying "John's not ashamed if he has another baby, now why should he sort of keep it secret?"

On 23 August, The Beatles played to a sell-out audience of 18,700 at the Hollywood Bowl in Los Angeles. The Hollywood Bowl was the last concert before The Beatles took a break in the tour. During the break they rented a house at 356 St Pierre Road in Bel Air and after the concert they held a party there. Guests at the party included actresses Sandra Dee and Jayne Mansfield. When asked, a few days before, if he would like to meet any American actresses Paul answered he'd like to meet Jayne Mansfield. When Jayne arrived, John was sat on a sofa bed with a lady friend. Long John Wade, a DJ from Hartford, made his way over to the couple. Pushing his microphone under the woman's nose he asked "And who might you be?" John punched the DJ's arm, sending the microphone flying. "Are you trying to start a scandal?" he asked furiously. Once John noticed Jayne he abandoned the woman and made his way over to her. John and Jayne spent the rest of the night together getting to know each other.

The next day, The Beatles attended a garden party held by Capitol Records president, Alan Livingston, at his Bel Air home. Guests at this party included Shelly Winters, Dean Martin, and Stan Freberg. On 25 August, The Beatles paid a visit to American actor Burt Lancaster at his home in LA. During the visit actress Jayne Mansfield turned up to the house with a male friend. Jayne made her way to John and tugging on his hair she asked, "Is it real?" John's response was to lower his eyes to her breasts and ask, "Well, are those real?" "There's only one way to find out" she told him. John offered to make cocktails and left the room to do so. He poured gin, vodka, red wine and various liqueurs into a mixer and then poured them into glasses. John was annoyed that Jayne hadn't turned up alone and before pouring Jayne's cocktail, he opened the mixer and pissed into it. After cocktails and a tarot card reading, Jayne invited the group to the famous Whiskey-A-Go-Go club. George, Ringo, Mal and Neil got into one car but Paul stayed behind with actress Peggy Lipton. John and Jayne left together, jumping into the back of a police car. They were joined by DJ Long John Wade who remembers they were "making out like kids". The paparazzi were out in force and George remembers "It seemed to take us twenty minutes to get from the door to the table." They had been tipped off by Jayne who wanted to have her photo taken with the group. Jayne was desperate to be romantically linked to one of the group.

In the club she sat herself in-between John and George. "She had her hands on our legs, by our groins" George remembers. She particularly wanted John. John spent most of the night trying to get rid of her. George, on the other hand, was more bothered about trying to get rid of the paparazzi and when one tried to take his photo he threw his drink over him. Two photos were taken, the first shows an angry George pointing at the photographer, the second shows him out of his seat, glass in head and if you look close enough you can see the liquid (reportedly melted ice) leaving the glass. It was this photo that made the papers and not the one Jayne had wanted. Shortly afterwards, The Beatles left, John and Jayne were hand in hand until they were separated by security leaving Jayne desperately struggling to get back to John.

Meanwhile, Paul was hooking up with nineteen-year-old Peggy Lipton. Peggy was an unknown actress that was freshly signed to Universal Studios. Peggy had been invited to Alan Livingston's party were she got to meet her crush Paul McCartney for the first time. "My God, you're beautiful" Paul told her as he took her hand. He led her to the piano where he played to her for a few minutes before taking her upstairs and kissing her. "I took a shower to slow things down" she wrote in her autobiography Breathing Out. Dressed in nothing but a towel, Peggy returned to Paul who began to caress her in one of the bedrooms. The towel fell to the floor and the couple made love. Peggy left the party feeling used but she'd given Paul her number and the next day he invited her to Burt Lancaster's house. While the other three Beatles went out with Jayne Mansfield to the Whiskey-A-Go-Go, Paul stayed at home with Peggy making love to her through the night. Peggy wasn't the only girl Paul slept with during that tour. Once back in the UK he bragged to his cousin, Mike Robbins, that one night he had shared his bed with three gorgeous blondes.

Brian and The Beatles were enjoying their trip to America as much as possible. On 28 August they met Bob Dylan at the Delmonico Hotel in New York. Bob introduced The Beatles and their manager to marijuana. That night, Bob Dylan, Bob's friend, Al Aronowitz, The Beatles, Brian Epstein, their roadie, Mal Evans and Peter Brown smoked one joint after another and giggled the night away. Drugs weren't the only thing getting smuggled into The Beatles' hotel rooms. American journalist, Larry Kane, spent a lot of time with the group while they toured America and he remembers The Beatles didn't sleep with groupies in America. The fans were too young and too much of a risk and The Beatles couldn't leave the hotel without being mobbed so instead the group's roadies, Mal Evans and Neil Aspinall, would bring prostitutes back to the hotel rooms. Larry remembers one night when eight or nine women were brought into the hotel and The Beatles and their entourage were told "Gentlemen, take your pick". Brian immediately walked out.

Brian, of course, wasn't interested in women. He'd been hanging around the gay bars in New York. One of those bars was Kelly's Bar on 45th Street between 6th Avenue and Broadway. Originally a famous serviceman's bar, it had now become known for the male hustlers who would hang out there. Brian and his friend and American business partner, Nat Weiss, would go there to pick up men. Another bar was a country and western bar called the Wagon Wheel. Across the street from Kelly's Bar, the Wagon Wheel was also a great place to pick up men. Its usual clientele was the rough types that Brian liked so much. One of the men Brian had picked up was a young Californian called Diz Gillespie.

Diz would became Brian's regular boyfriend for a time. Brian had had a boyfriend before, his first was an actor called Michael. According to Brian's houseman, Lonnie Trimble, Diz looked like singer-songwriter Gene Pitney. "A clean-cut sort of young man". Brian flew Diz back to London with him when The Beatles' tour ending in September. He then signed Diz as a NEMS artist and provided him with a new wardrobe and paid off his debts. Press announcements were sent out about Brian's "new discovery" and Diz started to receive an allowance. Diz moved into Brian's house with him and Lonnie remembers "It was like happy families" but it wasn't to last. Diz was bisexual and would often invite girls over to the flat while Brian was out. One day, Lonnie walked in to find the flat "all messed up with girls all over the place". Both Brian and Diz were enjoying a daily cocktail of drugs including uppers, Tainals and Cognal. Brian could easily afford to fund his drug habit, Diz, however, couldn't and he began stealing from Brian to pay for his drug habit and his behaviour lead to the couple having arguments and on occasion those arguments would lead to fistfights.

One evening Brian invited his parents over for dinner. Halfway through the meal Diz stood up, insulted Brian and walked out of the flat. Brian then got up and left too, leaving his parents feeling dumbfounded, sitting there not knowing what to do. They decided to get their coats and leave. Another argument ended with Brian ordering Diz out of his house. In a rage, Diz raced into the kitchen, grabbed the largest knife he could find and held it to Brian's throat. Diz demanded Brian emptied his wallet before leaving. Diz would eventually leave Brian for good on 1 April 1965. That morning he phoned Lonnie Trimble and his chauffeur, Alf Blackburn, to come in on their day off. Lonnie made Brian breakfast and when he came out of his room for it he told Lonnie "You can have everything and still be unhappy" before breaking down in tears. Lonnie put his arm around him and told him to "snap out of it". Brian decided to take his mind of Diz he would take a holiday to the south of France with Peter Brown, his personal assistant. One day, shortly after Diz left, Brian called Lonnie into his room to speak to him. "It was the first time I ever went into his bedroom when he was actually in bed" Lonnie remembers. Lonnie told Brian that Diz was now living in California and that Brian should leave him there "out of harm's way" but Brian had other plans. He told Lonnie that he was going to make Diz a star. "It was during the same discussion that he told me that he and John Lennon had been lovers" Lonnie recalls. A few weeks later Diz was back in London but it wasn't to last and it wasn't long before Diz was back in America.

Diz would reappear in Brian's life again in August 1965. Brian had arrived in New York two days ahead of The Beatles American tour. Diz was also in New York and had contacted Brian wanting to see him. Worried that Diz would do something to embarrass him or The Beatles, Brian agreed to meet Diz but asked Nat Weiss to help him get rid of him. Nat agreed to help, tracked down Diz and invited him to his office for a talk. "I had met thousands of him" Nat later said "He was the garden-variety type hustler. If you wanted to keep your beer cold you'd put it next to his heart." Diz told Nat that he loved Brian "I don't want anything from him" he told Nat "I just want to see him." Nat told Diz that he wasn't going to get anything from Brian and he wasn't going to get anywhere near him. Diz told Nat "Brian's got lots of money. If he wants me to stay away....well, if I had a car I could go away". Nat didn't want to give Diz a car knowing that giving him anything would only result in him returning for more but Brian insisted that Nat gave Diz $3,000 to buy a car. With the $3,000 Diz agreed to stay locked in a hotel room at the Warwick Hotel until The Beatles had left town. Nat even hired a private guard to stand outside Diz's hotel room.

Diz would make one last return a year later during The Beatles' last American tour in August 1966. The tour came to an end in California with a concert in Los Angeles followed by one the next day in San Francisco. The San Francisco concert would turn out to be the group's last. While in Los Angeles, Diz had called Brian and told him he loved him, he was in town and wanted to see him. Brian agreed and met Diz at a house in Beverly Hills that The Beatles had stayed in the year before. Brian gave Diz a tour of the house, showing him where The Beatles had slept before showing him the pool where they sat together talking and enjoying the sun. Other than Nat Weiss, they were alone, no servants, no press, no Beatles. Later in the day, Brian and Diz took a trip to a local supermarket to buy the items they needed for that night's dinner. Back at the Beverly Hills home Brian cooked roast chicken and vegetables for himself, Diz and Nat.

The next morning, Diz left early saying he had left his suitcase at the bungalow at the Beverly Hills Hotel. When Nat and Brian arrived at the bungalow later that morning they found Diz had gone and so had their attaché cases. Nat's case contained important business documents but Brian's case contained a large supply of pills, Polaroid photographs and a brown paper bag stuffed with $20,000. Nat said they should call the police but Brian wouldn't allow it, there was too much of a risk of a scandal if the press found out about Brian's drug habit and then what if they found out about his secret love life?

The next day, Brian flew back to England with The Beatles. When he returned he received a phone call from Nat Weiss who had received a blackmail letter to his office from Diz Gillespie. Diz was demanding an additional $10,000 for the return of Brian's photographs and letters. "Pay him the money" Brian told Nat "Just give him his bloody money." Nat however hired a private detective in Los Angeles and, without telling Brian, set up a phony ransom rendezvous with Diz. Diz however didn't turn up as Nat had hoped and instead sent a young accomplice. The accomplice was turned over to the police and agreed to lead them to the case if they promised to not press charges. The case still had $12,000 but no pills or letters and photos. Diz had taken $8,000 and disappeared. Brian now lived in constant fear that one day Diz would either blackmail him again or sell the letters and photographs to some newspaper. Diz never did and was never seen again. The fear of Diz's return worried Brian until his untimely death on 27 August 1967.

Diz wasn't the only person Brian had offered to make famous in return for sexual favours. John Gustafson, the bass player with The Merseybeats, remembers one night at a party at Brian's flat that Brian made a pass on him. The Merseybeats popularity was beginning to fade and John admits "I was pretty broke". At the end of the night, Brian put his arm around John and told him "You know, John, I can really help you if..." "The implied 'if' was there" John remembers but he wasn't interested, he told Brian "I know you can help me, Brian, but I can't really help you and I really have to go now". John left and never saw Brian again.

When The Beatles returned to England, after their American tour in 1964, they began work on their next album Beatles For Sale. At the time George was becoming closer to American actress Joey Heatherton. They had met during the group's US tour and stayed in touch via long-distance telephone calls. They phoned each other almost daily for around three months and it's rumoured that George wrote the song 'I Need You' about her. The song was written in February 1965 and released in August on the album Help! Meanwhile, Beatles For Sale was released on 4 December 1964 and included the song 'Every Little Thing'. The song was written by Paul at the Asher's family home and was inspired by his girlfriend, Jane Asher. The Beatles finished off the year with Another Beatles Christmas Show, a set of 40 shows that ran into January 1965. The compere for the shows was disc jockey Jimmy Savile. The Beatles had first met Jimmy Savile in 1961 when they played at the Three Coins club in Manchester which he co-owned. By 1964, he was presenting a new music chart television programme called Top of the Pops. In 2012, a year after his death, allegations of Jimmy Savile's sexual abuse of under-aged children came to light. Jimmy had allergy abused 450 victims over a period of four decades with the first allegation dating back to 1959. It is claimed that Jimmy had used his role as a DJ and television presenter to gain access to victims. Had Jimmy used his role as the compere of Another Beatles Christmas Show to gain access to under-aged Beatle fans? It is quite possible, not all the cases against Jimmy have become public. In an interview in 2012, Paul remembers "We [The Beatles] always thought there was something a little bit suspect." The Beatles were fond of teenage girls but never once did anyone under the age of sixteen enter a Beatles' bed. "We couldn't always be sure" Paul remembered in 2012 "but there was a definite no-no involved in under-age kids." He then added that the lads didn't have to worry because "there were plenty of over sixteen-year-olds."

Unfortunately for Paul, he and The Beatles have been associated with numerous other men that have at one time been accused of paedophilia and/or sexual abuse. Liverpudlian comedian Jimmy Tarbuck, who went to school with John Lennon, was arrested by North Yorkshire Police in April 2013 over an alleged sexual assault on a young boy in the 1970s. Rolf Harris, who like Savile, had been a compere on a Beatles' show and had recorded a version of 'Tie My Kangaroo Down Sport' for the BBC with The Beatles, was arrested in March 2013 over historical allegations of sexual offences. He was arrested again in August and was charged on nine counts of indecent assault dating to the 1980s and four counts of making indecent images a child in 2012.

'60s pop star Jonathan King, who had a hit with 'Everyone's Gone to the Moon' in 1965, was a friend of The Beatles and would often drink with them in nightclubs around London. He was arrested for sexual assault in November 2000 and again in January 2001. He was sentenced for three and half years for sexually assaulting five teenage boys in the 1980s. The lead singer of The Who, Pete Townshend, who had known Paul since the 1960s and worked with him in the 1970s and 1980s, was cautioned by the police in 2003 after he used a credit card to register with a website advertising child pornography. Rolling Stones bassist Bill Wyman had first met Paul in the 1960s and was friends with him throughout the '60s and '70s. He began his relationship with Mandy Smith in 1983, when she was just 13-years-old. In 2010, Mandy admitted that the relationship had been a sexual one and she first slept with Wyman when she was 14. The couple married in 1989, when Mandy was 18, Bill was 52. They divorced in 1991.

Liverpudlian comedian Freddie Starr, who had a singing career in the 1960s and 1970s, shared the bill with The Beatles in 1963, when he fronted The Midnighters. He was arrested in November 2012 in connection with the Jimmy Savile sexual abuse scandal. He had been accused of molesting a 14-year-old girl in 1974. He was arrested a second time in April 2013 over new allegations of sexual abuse. DJ Chris Denning, who had worked with The Beatles several times during the 1960s, was first arrested for gross indecency and indecent assault in 1974. He was imprisoned for 18 months for gross indecency with a child in 1985 and in 1988 he was jailed for three years for indecent assault on a 13-year-old boy. In 1996, he was imprisoned for 10 weeks for publishing indecent photographs. He was part of a group of child sex offenders based around a disco for young people in Surrey that included Jonathan King. He was jailed for five years on charges of producing child pornography. In June 2013, he was arrested in East London as part of Operation Yewtree. Another BBC DJ and self-appointed 'Beatles expert', John Peel, had first meet The Beatles in the late sixties and stayed in touch with them throughout the seventies and eighties. After his death in 2004, allegations were made that Peel had had sexual relationships with girls as young as 13 in the late sixties and early seventies. He married his first wife, Shirley Anne Milburn, in 1965 when she was just 15, he was 26. It's no wonder then that his favourite song was 'Teenage Kicks'.

Glam Rock star Gary Gliter was arrest in November 1997 after pornographic images of children were discovered on the hard drive of his laptop. He was also accused with having sex with a 14-year-old girl and was charged in 1999. After his release he moved to Cambodia where he lived until 2002. He was then deported to Vietnam due to suspected child sexual abuse and in 2005 he was arrested by Vietnamese authorities and charged with molesting two under aged girls and was sentenced in 2006. Gliter was arrested again in October 2012 after being accused of having sex with teenage girls in the 1970s. Paul met Glitter a number of times during the 1970s and appeared on stage with him in 1996.

Michael Jackson befriended Paul in the 1980s which resulted in the pair writing and recording together. He was accused of sexually abusing a 13-year-old boy in 1993. The civil suit was settled out of court with Michael paying $22,000,000 to the boy's family. He was accused of sexually abusing another 13-year-old boy in 2003 but in 2005 the jury found him not guilty on all charges. Since his death in 2009, choreographer Wade Robson has claimed that he was sexually abused by Michael for seven years in the 1990s but many doubt his claims. Was

Paul McCartney or any of the other Beatles part of a celebrity paedophile ring? It seems unlikely but Paul has no doubt been associated with several people accused of sexual crimes against children. Paul has denied ever sleeping with anyone under aged but John had admitted to coming close to it on more than one occasion. If any of The Beatles had slept with under aged girls it's fair to say it was never intentional but it would also be fair to claim that rock 'n' roll and paedophilia has gone hand in hand since its early days in the 1950s.

Elvis Presley had first met his wife-to-be Priscilla Wagner in 1959, when she was only fourteen. Jerry Lee Lewis married his first cousin once removed, Myra Brown, in 1958, when the girl was only 13-years-old. Chuck Berry, the writer of 'Sweet Little Sixteen', was arrested in December 1959 and was questioned over allegations of having sex with a 14-year-old girl. He was fined $5,000, and sentenced to five years in prison. Presley, Lewis and Berry were all heroes of The Beatles and their music had a massive influence on the group.

Attitudes towards paedophilia in the fifties and sixties were very different to the attitude we take today. It wasn't that people didn't care but the general public were so ignorant towards paedophilia that it had even become part of pop culture. Just a quick look at some hit songs from the time shows that. Johnny Burnette's hit 'You're Sixteen' from 1961 is an obvious one with the 28-year-old Burnette singing about his 16-year-old girlfriend-'You're sixteen, you're beautiful and you're mine.' Ringo liked the song so much he later recorded his own version. 1962 saw Steve Lawrence releasing 'Go Away Little Girl' which was covered by The Happenings in 1966. Meanwhile, in 1965 The Lovin Spoonful sang 'Younger Girl' on their debut album. Neil Diamond sang 'Girl, You'll Be a Woman Soon' in 1967 but perhaps the most disturbing song in this weird trend was Traffic's 1968 song 'Vagabond Virgin' which tells the tale of a 13-year-old girl losing her virginity. The best known song about an older man lusting after a young girl has to be the number one hit for Gary Puckett & The Union Gap-'Young Girl'. The song, which includes the lyrics 'young girl, get out of my mind. My love for you is way out of line', was released in 1968. The following year Blind Faith released their self-titled debut album which featured a topless, pubescent girl on the cover. Lennon and McCartney did not shy away from this trend and influenced by songs of the fifties like 'Sweet Little Sixteen', 'Hey Little Girl', and 'Little Bitty Pretty One', the duo wrote their own songs about young lovers. Beatle songs like 'Hello Little Girl', 'I Lost My Little Girl', 'Little Child', 'I Saw Her Standing There', and the Wings B-side, 'Girls' School', all fit into this category.

 It should be noted that not all the men mentioned in this chapter have been charged for the crimes they have been accused of and some have been found not guilty.

7

Norwegian Wood

Once Another Beatles Christmas Show had ended on 16 January 1965, the Lennons decided to take a holiday and on 25 January they flew out to St Moritz, Switzerland with The Beatles' producer, George Martin and his girlfriend, Judy Lockhart-Smith. It was during this trip the John had an affair with an unknown woman. She invited him back to her apartment which was decorated in cheap pine and they stayed up until two in the morning, drinking wine and chatting before going to bed together. John wrote about the affair in the song 'Norwegian Wood (This Bird Has Flown)' which was later released on Rubber Soul. He began writing the song on his acoustic guitar during the two week holiday but changed some of the details. The pine became Norwegian wood which sounded better and the end of the tale was changed so the Cyn wouldn't find out about the affair.

In the song, John says he went off to sleep in the bath. Of course, the reality was different. "I was very careful and paranoid because I didn't want my wife, Cyn, to know that there really was something going on outside of the household" he said later. The last verse about burning the house down was added later after John returned to England and asked Paul to help him finish the song. John would later say he couldn't remember who the woman in the song was but his friend Pete Shotton suggests that it was a journalist that John had been close to. It's possible it could have been Maureen Cleave, a journalist who interviewed John and The Beatles several time, but Maureen claims she's never slept with John.

According to author Philip Norman, John had an affair with German-born model Sonny Freeman for over a year and it was her that he was writing about. Sonny was married to photographer Robert Freeman who worked with The Beatles, taking the photos for the covers of With The Beatles, Beatles For Sale, Help! and Rubber Soul. The Freemans lived in the flat below the Lennons at 13 Emperor's Gate and the two couples would often socialise together. John would turn up at the Freeman's flat when Robert was out and he and Sonny would stay up all night, drinking wine and talking. It was then that the affair started and it continued under the noses of both Cyn and Robert until 1965. It should also be noted that the lounge of the Freeman's flat was lined with wooden panels.

'Norwegian Wood' wasn't the only Beatles song about sex. In 1966, Time Magazine claimed that 'Day Tripper' was about a prostitute (not quite right) and that 'Norwegian Wood' was about a lesbian (totally wrong). When asked about the magazine's claims in a press conference Paul remarked, "We were just trying to write songs about lesbians and prostitutes". Later in the same press conference one reporter asks what 'Eleanor Rigby' is about to which John jokes, "Two queers....two barrel boys".

A closer listen to 'Please Please Me' would suggest that the song is about sex or the lack off: 'Please, please me, oh yeah, like I please you.' John's first book, In His Own Write, was published in 1964. One of the stories, No Flies On Frank, tell of how a man, Frank, wakes up one morning to find his penis has grown an extra 12 inches. After an argument with his wife, Frank uses his extra-large penis to beat her to death. The original lyrics to 'Day Tripper' were much ruder until Paul convinced John to change them. When he first played his new song to the band the lyrics went: 'She's a prick teaser, she took me half the way there.' In the song 'Girl' The Beatles can be heard in the background chanting 'tit, tit, tit, tit'. The woman in the song 'Drive My Car' claims that one day she is going to be a star and offers to show a man 'a better time' if he becomes her chauffeur. The song 'Love You To' from Revolver contains the lyrics 'I'll make love to you, if you want me to' and 'make love all day long'. 'Penny Lane' mentions 'finger pies'-Liverpublian slang for pleasuring a girl. 'I Am The Walrus' was banned by the BBC for having the line 'You let your knickers down' while 'All Together Now' asks 'Can I take my friend to bed?'. 'A Day In The Life' from the Sgt. Pepper's album includes the line 'I love to turn you on' while the run-out groove of the same album contains a hidden message if played backwards-'We'll fuck you like Supermen'. While many have claimed that's not what's being said, Paul McCartney has admitted it is there. 'I've Got a Feeling' from the album Let It Be contains the lyric 'Everybody had a wet dream'. And as for 'Why Don't We Do It In The Road', well, that's just obvious. The Beatles were about more than just holding hands and 'I'm Happy Just to Dance With You'. There's more of course, for example, the Wings single 'Hi Hi Hi' was banned by the BBC for its sexually suggestive lyrics. But let's not go into the meanings of songs too much or we'll end up in 'Paul is dead' territory.

Better known today as being the pop impresario who discovered Genesis, the Bay City Rollers, and 10CC, in the mid-sixties, Jonathan King was a pop star in his own right. His first hit, 'Everyone's Gone to the Moon', was released in 1965. King's London apartment was the scene of many far out parties during the swinging sixties. In his autobiography, '65 My Life So Far', he claims that John Lennon had slept over at the apartment "two or three times" with several young ladies, plenty of booze and the best weed money could buy. King claims John was perfectly happy to indulge in multi-gender sessions of sexual stimulation. Sixties singer and later television presenter, Gloria Hunniford, tells an even more shocking story about Lennon's sexuality that took place in 1965. Gloria and her friend attended a party in London that a number of London's biggest names also attended including John Lennon.

Wondering around the house, Gloria and her friend opened a door that led to a bedroom. To their shock they saw John having anal sex with a well-known male celebrity photographer. The girls quickly closed the door and kept what they had seen a secret for almost forty years.

Ringo Starr was the second Beatle to get married. Maureen Cox was born in Liverpool on 4 August 1946 and was the only child of Joseph and Florence Cox. After leaving school at the age of fourteen, she became a trainee hairdresser at Ashley du Pre in Liverpool. She had been dating Ringo since 1962 but when The Beatles moved to London in the summer of 1963, Maureen stayed in Liverpool. Ringo was dating Paula Bennett at the time and later he would date Vicki Hodge. Vicki was a seventeen-year-old London born model when she first met Ringo and they dated until June 1964. When Ringo had his tonsils taken out, Maureen come down to London to be by his side and Ringo had to call it off with all of his London girlfriends. Maureen spent that Christmas with Ringo, Vicki Hodge went on holiday to Sweden and when she returned in the New Year she found Maureen had left Liverpool and moved to London. The couple lived at 34 Montagu Square and in late January eighteen-year-old Maureen found herself pregnant.

Ringo did the "right thing" and on 20 January he proposed to Maureen at the Ad-Lib Club. Because she was pregnant, Brian Epstein arranged for the wedding to take place as soon as possible. It was important that the couple were married before it became obvious that Maureen was pregnant and the wedding took place just three weeks after the couple had got engaged. They were married at Caxton Hall Register Office on 11 February 1965. The wedding was attended by Brian, John and George. Paul was in Tunisia at the time and could not attend. George joked "Two down, two to go".

The newlyweds had a three day honeymoon at Brian's lawyer, David Jacobs', holiday home in Hove. They couldn't escape the press however and were besieged by reporters and photographers. On the first day of their honeymoon the couple spent a couple of minutes in the back garden speaking with reporters. "Are you going to get a honeymoon?" one reporter asks. "No I don't think so" Ringo replies "not with the likes of you chaps around". "Are you thinking of a honeymoon?" he asks not getting the hint. "This was supposed to be it" Ringo tells him "but it didn't work". Still not taking the hint the reporter asks "How long was it supposed to be?" Ringo tells him he'll be back at "work" on Monday. Later, the reporter asks where Paul is but Ringo says he won't tell him adding "he might as well have a bit of peace, I'm not getting any".

Maureen and Ringo soon became the most social Beatle couple. They enjoyed dancing and drinking at their favourite London nightclubs, going to see the latest movies and visiting the gambling clubs that Brian Epstain also frequented. They often held parties and hung out with their celebrity friends at fancy restaurants. The couple's first child, Zak, was born 13 September 1965 and a second son, Jason, followed on 19 August 1967 with a daughter, Lee Parkin, being born on 17 November 1970.

Eleven days after the wedding, The Beatles began filming their second film, Help!, in the Bahamas. In March, filming took the group to Austria. They spent 12 days filming in the town of Obertauern staying at the Hotel Edelweiss. Despite being with his wife, Cyn, John couldn't resist sleeping with the local women. While Cyn was in one room, John would be in another sleeping with women that had been handpicked for him by Neil and Mal. One of those women was twenty-eight-year-old Marion Hagel. Despite being married herself, Marion had not turned down the offer to sleep with a Beatle and when she arrived at the hotel it was John who picked her out of the line-up. Shortly after The Beatles returned to England, Marion found herself pregnant and in October she gave birth to a baby girl who she named Kristina.

When she was twelve, Kristina was told by Marion that her father was John Lennon. The truth had been kept a secret because Marion was now living in a quiet middle-class area of Hamburg and was still married to Karl Hagel. In 1994, Kristina turned up in Liverpool, claiming she was John's secret daughter. She met up with John's Uncle Charlie who was convinced and she produced a birth certificate that had John Winston Lennon as her father. She even claimed that John had visited her once in

Germany when she was a toddler and gave her a child's pedal car shaped like a Volkswagen Beetle. The birth certificate was proven to be fake and her real one showed her father as being 'Karl August Egon Hagel'-her mother's husband.

Appearing alongside The Beatles in Help! was actress Eleanor Bron. The twenty-seven-year-old actress was playing the part of Ahme and during filming she struck up a friendship with John. The two friends started spending time together, drinking in hotel bars and discussing politics and philosophy. In a 2007 interview with Mojo magazine Eleanor remembers "He was attracted to women who knew more than he did or who were older whom he thought he could learn from." They became lovers and one night John took Eleanor out for a meal "which was very nice of him" Eleanor said in 2007. They found a tiny restaurant where the pair were "only just not recognised." Eleanor, who had a boyfriend at the time, has denied that they were lovers but John would later admit that in fact they did have an affair during 1965. The last time Eleanor saw John was when The Beatles played at the Hollywood Bowl in August 1965. Eleanor was staying in Beverly Hills at the time and turned up back stage to spend some time with John.

In August 1965, The Beatles returned to America for the third time. They played sixteen shows over eleven nights, crisscrossing the country and having sex with as many women as possible. When the group landed in New York at the beginning of the tour on 15 August, the group's roadies, Mal and Neil, set about finding some girls for themselves and The Beatles. Among them was fourteen-year-old Geraldine Smith. She was walking down MacDougal Street when she was approached by Rolling Stone Bill Wyman's girlfriend Francesca Overman. "How would you like to meet The Beatles?" she asked. Geraldine didn't believe her but went along with it anyway just in case it turned out to be true. It was true and Geraldine soon found herself sat in the back of a car with a group of other girls and a New York Post reporter, Al Aronowitz. The car took the girls to the Warwick Hotel where four stoned Beatles ate steak and baked potatoes. Afterwards they played spin the bottle and when the boys picked out which girls they wanted to take back to their room, Geraldine was asked if she'd prefer to sleep with John or Paul. Geraldine confessed that she was only fourteen and still a virgin and that night she slept on the floor wrapped in an American flag.

Six days later, when The Beatles came to Minneapolis, Paul McCartney was almost arrested. The police enforced a curfew of midnight for anyone under eighteen. The Beatles were staying at the Leamington Motor Inn and had already packed a room full of women-prostitutes, groupies and fans. Two of the women slept with every man in sight in the hope they would eventually make their way to The Beatles. In the morning, butt naked, the two women ran into the lobby screaming "Rape!" The police arrived and began checking the ID of the girls in the group's rooms before escorting them out of the hotel. When they tried to enter Paul's room he refused to unlock the door. Brian Epstein was called and informed Paul that the police were threatening him with arrest. Paul backed down, the girl in his room had an ID that showed her age as being twenty-one but as the police inspector told the press "I doubt she is older than sixteen"

On 23 August, the band began a five day break from touring. Actress Zsa Zsa Gabor rented the group her house at 2850 Benedict Canyon Drive in Beverly Hills. That evening they attended a party held at the home of Capitol Records' president Alan Livingstone. Among the guests, that included Jane Fonda, Groucho Marx, and Dean Martin, was Hayley Mills, who was excited to be reunited with George. The next day, The Beatles held a party of their own. The guests included Eleanor Bron, Roger McGuinn and David Crosby of The Byrds, Daily Mirror newspaper journalist Don Short, actor Peter Fonda, Peter Yarrow, from Peter, Paul and Mary and folk singer Joan Baez. During the party John, George and Ringo all took LSD along with Roger McGuinn and David Crosby. They played music together and talked about their favourite songs. Peter Fonda, who had accidently shot himself in the stomach and had almost died when he was eleven, was showing off his bullet wound and telling everybody "I know what it's like to be dead". His words would later end up in the song 'She Said, She Said'. Later they swam in the pool, ate a meal (which John, high on acid, ate with his hands) and watched the film Cat Ballou starring Jane Fonda. As the party came to an end the guests left but John asked Joan Baez to stay with the group for the remainder of The Beatles' stay in Los Angeles. The house did not have enough bedrooms for everyone so, John offered Joan his bed saying he would sleep on the floor but, as Joan remembers, John's bed was "the size of a small swimming pool" so Joan suggested that they shared the bed. Joan went to sleep and a few hours later, John got into bed with her. John woke her up wanting sex. "John" she said "I'm probably as tired as you are, and I don't want you to feel you have to perform on my behalf" and they both went to sleep. John would later list Joan among the numerous affairs he had during the sixties, a claim that Joan denied in a 1983 interview in Rolling Stone. Of course, John and Joan spent three other nights together and in October, John added the Donovan single 'Turquoise' to his jukebox. Turquoise had been written about Joan by Scottish folk singer Donovan who was madly in love with her at the time. Joan would later cover the song herself in 1967.

Another night during The Beatles L.A break, Paul got in contact with Peggy Lipton, who he had met the previous year, and invited her over for dinner. John found the entire situation amusing. He couldn't understand why Paul was making an effort with

Peggy and taking things seriously when he could just have sex with her, or in fact, any girl, at the drop of a hat. The truth was Paul really liked Peggy and was considering leaving Jane Asher for her.

As far as the fans and the media were concerned Paul and Jane Asher were in a happy relationship together and if you believed the rumours they were to get married any day. They had been on a ten day holiday to Tunisia in February 1965 and in May they spent a fortnight together in Portugal. Behind closed doors, things weren't so happy. Jane was busy pursuing her successful acting career but Paul wanted her to stay at home like the girls back in working-class Liverpool. While Jane was appearing in Great Expectations at the Theatre Royal in Bristol in November 1965, she refused to answer Paul's calls. Jane ignoring him influenced Paul to write 'You Won't See Me' which was recorded on 11 November. Other arguments lead to Jane leaving Paul for a while and Paul wrote 'I'm Looking Through You' which was recorded the same day as 'You Won't See Me'. Both songs were released on Rubber Soul in December. Released the same day was the double A-side single 'Day Tripper'/'We Can Work It Out'. 'We Can Work It Out' was another of Paul's songs about Jane. During her time away from Paul, Jane had been seeing other men but it worked both ways and Jane wasn't the only woman in Paul's life.

He first met folk singer Julie Felix in 1965, after the release of her second album and the two started dating in secret. They dated on and off throughout 1965 but their relationship came to an end in January 1966, when Julie married David John Evans. By the end of the year Julie and David had broken up and Julie returned to Paul. Paul played Julie 'Penny Lane' and 'Strawberry Fields Forever' in December before they were released as a double A-side in February 1967. Julie was also at Paul's side when The Beatles filmed the promo films for 'Penny Lane', 'A Day In The Life' and 'Strawberry Fields Forever' in the first week of February 1967.

When The Beatles returned to America in 1966 for what would become there last ever tour their opening act was The Ronettes. Phil Spector, The Ronettes' manager and boyfriend of lead singer, Ronnie Bennett, was so worried that Ronnie would cheat on him with John Lennon that he refused to allow her to take part in the tour. Instead he replaced her with her cousin Elaine Mayes. Backstage, George could get together with Ronnie's sister Estelle. The last time they had seen each other was in February 1964 but George was ill in bed with flu. Despite the number of celebrity lovers the group now had, the number of groupies hadn't decreased but it was now roadies, Derek and Neil, who were getting most of the action. The girls would sit in a hotel room waiting for their turn to sleep with one of the group. Mal and Neil would 'audition' the girls first before they were taken to one of The Beatles' rooms. Not all the girls got to sleep with a Beatles and some would find themselves sleeping with Mal or Neil and then being sent away feeling used and betrayed.

In May 1966, Bob Dylan brought his world tour to England. During the tour, scenes for the documentary film, Eat The Document, were filmed. The tour ended with two nights at the Royal Albert Hall in London. Before the last night, on 27 May, Bob paid John a visit at his house in Weybridge, Surrey. Later, they drove to the Mayfair Hotel in London, where Bob was staying. During the trip, Bob and John were filmed chatting in the back of the limousine. During the conversation John asks Bob about the group The Mamas and The Papas. "I believe you're backing them" he says. Bob replies with "you're just interested in the big one, the big chick, right? You're just interested in the big chick. She' got a hold on you too!" Bob was referring to Cass Elliot, who John had a crush on. John quickly changed the subject. John would get to meet Cass in August of that year when The Beatles came to America. Cass had turned up to The Beatles' hotel one day and John wasted no time in taken her to his room where the couple made love. It wouldn't be long until the pair met up again. During a break in the tour, the group were visited by their former press officer, Derek Taylor. The Beatles were staying at a house rented by Brian Epstein at 7655 Curson Terrace in Beverly Hills. Derek had brought along members of some of the groups he was now working for including The Byrds and The Mamas and The Papas. John quickly took Cass into his room and the pair made love for hours. When The Mamas and The Papas came to London in late 1966, she was keen to meet up with John again and they spent the night at the Ad Lib club getting high on STP, a psychedelic drug. Mama Cass and John would see each other a handful of times throughout the sixties and seventies and it's rumoured that when she died in July 1974, Cass Elliot was pregnant with John's child.

8

Fuck Day

On Christmas Day 1965, George Harrison proposed to his girlfriend, Pattie Boyd. The happy couple then drove from their home, Kinfauns in Esher, to Brian Epstein's house in Chapel Street. While Pattie waited outside in the car, George went in to talk to Brian-George needed Brian's permission before the wedding could go ahead. Brian gave his blessing and ensured George he could arrange for the wedding to take place the following month. When George returned to the car he told Pattie "It's all right. Brian has said we can get married in January. Off we go!" Pattie's response was "God has spoken!"

When John found out he remarked "January's a bit soon. She must be in the club". The couple married on 21 January 1966 at Epsom Registry Office in Upper High Street in Esher, Surrey but John was wrong, Pattie was not pregnant. Paul McCartney and Brian Epstein shared best man duties while John and Ringo were on holiday in Trinidad with their wives. The next day, they held a press conference in London and on 8 February they began their honeymoon in Barbados, taking along Brian Epstein for the trip.

Pattie Boyd was born in Sommerset on 17 March 1944 but spent a lot of her childhood and early teens in Kenya. She had worked as a hairdresser before becoming a model. She did an advertisement for Smiths Crisps which was directed by Richard Lester, who later gave her her part in A Hard Day's Night. After her marriage to George, he insisted she gave up her career and she was rarely seen outside the house. When she did adventure outside, she risked being physically attacked by female fans who she called "horrible little girls".

While George and Pattie were madly in love, Paul and Jane were still having problems and despite a two week holiday in Switzerland, Paul moved out of the Asher home in March and moved into 7 Cavendish Avenue in St John's Wood, which he had bought the previous year. While in Switzerland, Paul had wrote a song called 'Why Did It Die?' which he later renamed 'For No One'. A few months later he wrote 'Here, There and Everywhere' while sat beside John Lennon's pool at his home in Weybridge. Both songs were about Jane and both would appear on The Beatles seventh album Revolver in August.

In 1966, touring for The Beatles had become dangerous, even life-threatening. In Japan they received death threats from right-wing Japanese nationalists who were protesting against the group performing at the Nippon Budokan in Tokyo, which was built for staging the martial arts. In the Philippines they snubbed the nation's first lady, Imelda Marcos, which led to all the group's security being removed and the group and their entourage being attacked at the airport. In America John's "More popular than Jesus" remark had caused so much upset in the deep south that mass book and album burnings were held and the Ku Klux Klan treated to put an end to The Beatles concerts. When a firecracker went off on the stage at the Memphis show on 19 August, everyone feared the worse and, thinking someone had been shot, all four Beatles spun round to face the other three. Nobody fell down dead and the concert continued. After their concert at Candlestick Park in San Francisco on 29 August, The Beatles decided they would end touring for good. An end to touring meant that the number of sexual partners the group had decreased dramatically but, despite three of the four members now being married, the affairs continued.

In November 1966, Japanese artist Yoko Ono held an exhibition at the Indica Gallery in London. John Lennon was invited to the preview on 9 November by the gallery's owner John Dunbar. John didn't normally make an effort to attend such events, but after hearing rumours that there would be orgies taking place inside giant bags, his mind was made up. John and Yoko hit it off from the start. When John first met Yoko she handed him a card that said 'Breathe'. John started to pant heavily "like this?" he asked "Yeah that's right" she replied. At that moment John Dunbar turned up and introduced the pair. John noticed a blank board with a hammer on a string and a box of nails. A sign read 'Hammer a Nail In'. John asked Yoko if he could hammer in the first nail, "It will cost you five shillings" she told him, not wanted to ruin the board before the opening night. "I'll give you an imaginary five shillings and hammer an imaginary nail in" was his reply. Yoko liked the idea and wanted to see John again. There was no orgies in bags that night but John liked Yoko, or at least as an artist.

The idea that Yoko didn't know who The Beatles were when she met John seems very unlikely. The group were very big in both the USA and Japan and most of the world for that matter. The Beatles were in newspapers, on magazine and book covers, on TV and the radio, they appeared in films and live on stage across the globe. It seems impossible that anyone could be unaware of The Beatles in 1966 and Yoko most likely made up the story to impress John. Oddly, Brian Epstein had also claimed to have not heard of The Beatles before 1961, despite them being one of the biggest bands in Liverpool, playing regular gigs at the Cavern-a club less than 5 minutes' walk from the NEMS store were Brian worked and the group constantly appearing in MesreyBeat-a newspaper stocked by NEMS that Brian wrote for. All that and the fact that The Beatles were always in NEMS, listening to records but never buying them. Decades later, Heather Mills would make a similar claim when she said she wasn't familiar with most of Paul's solo work. But let's get back to John and Yoko. John Lennon wasn't even the first Beatle Yoko Ono had met, Paul McCartney was.

Yoko Ono was born on 18 February 1933 in Tokyo, Japan. Her father, Eisuke, was a banker and her mother, Isoko Yasuda, was the great-granddaughter of Zenjiro Yasuda of the Yasuda banking family. In 1940, the family moved to New York but moved back to Japan in 1941. They moved back to New York after the war and Yoko enrolled into Sarah Lawrence College. In 1956, she married Japanese avant-garde music composer Toshi Ichiyanagi but by 1962 they had been living apart for several years and they filed for divorce that year. Before the divorce came through Yoko married Tony Cox on 28 November 1962. She had met Tony in 1961, after he had seen some of her art work in an anthology in New York. He tracked her down and found her living unhappily in Tokyo with Toshi. She had attempted suicide several times and had ended up in hospital after taking a drug overdose. Tony had visited Yoko in hospital and even moved in with her and Toshi. Tony and Yoko's marriage was annulled on 1 March 1963, but after her divorce came through the couple re-married on 6 June that year.

By that time Yoko was seven months pregnant with Tony's child. Their daughter, Kyoko Chan Cox, was born 8 August 1963. Tony and Kyoko returned to New York in 1964 with Yoko following in November. In New York she then became involved with the avant-garde group called Fluxus.

In 1966, Tony and Yoko came to London. Interested in the London art scene, she took trips to the Indica and an opening for the sculptor Claes Oldenburg. At the opening she met Paul McCartney, who she hoped would organise an exhibition for her. A few days later she turned up at Paul's home at Cavendish Avenue. She wanted to know if Paul had any spare manuscripts of Beatles lyrics that she could present to her friend and composer, John Cage, for his 55th birthday. (Many sources claim the manuscripts were collected for Cage's 50th birthday. This is untrue however due to the fact that Cage was born 5 September 1912 making him 50 in 1962 and 55 in 1967). Paul took her up to his room and the two made love. Paul told Yoko he didn't have any spare manuscripts but maybe John did. The pair came down stairs grinning, Paul walked Yoko to the door where he hugged her before she left. Yoko eventually got her Beatle lyrics by turning up at Abbey Road Studios but she wouldn't get to meet John for another month.

By 1967, London was in full swing and The Beatles were at the centre of it. For a short time drugs, free love, and rock and roll ruled the world. There seemed to be nonstop parties. Drug fuelled sex parties were a part of the culture as much as psychedelic music and hippie clothing. On 7 February 1967, The Beatles held a party at Abbey Road. Among the guests were Micky Dolenz of The Monkees, Paul's lover Julie Felix, and John's lover Cass Elliot. After the party Micky Dolenz was inspired to write the song 'Randy Scouse Git'. The song refers to The Beatles as 'The four kings of EMI'.

Later that month, Keith Richards of The Rolling Stones held a party at his Redlands home in Sussex. Among the guests were Mick Jagger, his girlfriend Marianne Faithfull, George Harrison and his wife Pattie Boyd. Marianne Faithfull had slept with three of the Stones despite being married to the artist John Dunbar. Marrianne had married John in May 1965, when she was three months pregnant with his child. In November, she gave birth to a son, Nicholas. She then left John for Mick Jagger, who she had decided was the best of the three Rolling Stones she had slept with. John and Marrianne finally divorced in 1970. During the 60s and early 70s, Marrianne had many songs written about her including 'Carrie Anne' by The Hollies (1967), 'You Can't Always Get What You Want' (1969), 'Wild Horses' (1971) and 'I Got the Blues' (1971) all by The Rolling Stones. But it was John Lennon who first wrote about Marrianne in The Beatles song 'And Your Bird Can Sing' which was released in 1966 on Revolver.

During the Redlands party, Sussex police carried out a drug raid on the building. They had been tipped off by the News of The World, who had in turn been tipped off by Keith Richard's chauffeur. Very few drugs were actually found at the party but what was found was enough to have Mick Jagger and Keith Richards arrested. When the police arrived, Marrianne had just got out of the bath and had wrapped herself in a fur rug. Rumour has it that Marrianne flashed the police. Another rumour involves a Mars Bar. One version says that Mick Jagger was using the chocolate bar as a sex toy on Marrianne, while another says he was eating the chocolate bar from between her legs. Everyone involved in the rumour including Mick, Marrianne, Keith, and the police who carried out the raid have all claimed the rumours to be untrue. George and Pattie had left the party a few minutes before the police arrived.

Later that year, John Lennon attended a party held by Eric Burdon of The Animals. During the party Eric and John were talking about the women they had slept with. Eric told John that he preferred black women and told him about his ex-girlfriend, Doreen Caulker, a black woman he had dated in the early sixties, who he wrote the song 'For Miss Caulker' for. He then told John about a Jamaican woman called Sylvia, who had introduced him to the pleasures of oral sex using a raw egg. Later that night, as the party turned into a drug fuelled orgy, John urged Eric on by shouting "Go on, go get it, egg man. Go for it". 'The Eggman' would later appear in The Beatles B-side 'I Am The Walrus'.

The Beatles spent most of the first three months of 1967 recording what would become the album Sgt. Pepper's Lonely Hearts Club Band. On 19 May, Brian Epstein held a party at his home in Chapel Street to celebrate the launch of the album. Among the guest was rock photographer Linda Eastman. Linda had photographed major stars including Janis Joplin, Jim Morrison, and Pete Townshend. Linda Louise Eastman was born in Scarsdale, New York on 24 September 1942. Her father, Lee Eastman, was the attorney for songwriter Jack Lawrence. Jack Lawrence would write the song 'Linda' for her the year she was born but the song wasn't published until 1946, when it was recorded by Ray Noble and Buddy Clark. The song has since been covered by Perry Como, Bing Crosby, King Curtis, Willie Nelson, Frank Sinatra, and Jan and Dean. She attended Scarsdale High School and graduated in 1959. She then began studying fine-arts at the University of Arizona, where she met Joseph Melvin See Jr. In 1962, her mother, Louise, died in a plane crash which gave Linda a fear of flight for the rest of her life. That same year she married Joseph, better known as Mel and their daughter, Heather, was born in December. The couple divorced in 1965 and Linda began working as a rock photographer. She first met The Beatles in 1966 when they played at Shea Stadium. She would next met Paul McCartney on 15 May 1967 at the Bag O'Nails nightclub in London. Linda was in London taking photos for J.Marks' book 'Rock and Other Four Letter Words' at the time. That night she was at the Bag O'Nails with Chas Chandler of The Animals, when she was approached by Paul. Paul asked Linda if she wanted to go to another club with him and the couple left for the Speakeasy. They met again four days later at the Sgt. Pepper's launch party but that night Linda left with the other photographers and a whole year would pass before she met Paul again.

With Linda back in America, Paul began an affair with Marijke Koger. Marijke was one half of Dutch design collective known as The Fool. Made up of Marijke and her boyfriend, Simon Posthuma, The Fool had first come to London in 1966 and became involved with The Beatles through Brian Epstein. Marijke became a regular visitor to Paul's home on Cavendish Avenue and would give him private tarot readings. One thing led to another and the couple ended up in bed together. The affair continued until August when one day, having guested at what was going on, Simon turned up at Cavendish Avenue and questioned Paul. Paul admitted to the affair saying that he couldn't help it. He told Simon that Jane already knew and there was no need to tell her. She didn't of course, Paul was simply covering his own back. Paul ended the affair there and then and the three remained friends. Paul's next affair took place in October 1967. Elisabeth Aronsson was a young Swedish model who had had an affair with Roger Daltrey of The Who which had resulted in her giving birth to a son, Mathias, in 1967. Later that year, on 14 October, when Paul and George flew out to Sweden to partake in a private meditation course with the Maharishi Mahesh Yogi, Elisabeth was by Paul's side and they were photographed together. They returned to England on the 17 October.

Paul and Jane's relationship had hit a new low and the couple tried several times to rekindle the love they had once known. In April, Paul flew to America to surprise Jane on her birthday. Then, in July, the couple flew out to Athens for a holiday with the other Beatles. It seemed to have worked and on Christmas day 1967, Jane and Paul announced their engagement.

Being engaged didn't stop Paul from seeing other

women and it was around this time that he began seeing Graciela Borges. Graciela was an Argentine actress in her mid-twenties and was living in London at the time. "We had an excellent relationship" she remembered later. Graciela and Paul dated for around a year but she won't go into details.

Meanwhile, John was seeing a lot more of Yoko. Throughout 1966 and 1967, Yoko had been appearing frequently in the press due to her controversial art events. She filmed 365 people's naked bottoms for the film Bottoms in 1966 and in June 1967, she was arrested in Belgium, along with Tony Cox, for dancing naked in public and in August, dressed in a bag, she tied herself to a lion in Trafalgar Square. Her next meeting with John came on 29 April 1967, when Yoko was performing at the 14 Hour Technicolour Dream, the benefit party for the underground newspaper International Times being held at Alexandra Palace in London. That night John Lennon had invited John Dunbar over to his house to drop acid. As the pair sat watching TV they saw a news report about the event and decided to attend. Yoko now had her heart set on John and she made the next move. She sent John a copy of her book Grapefruit, which had been published in 1964. John liked the book so much that he then invited Yoko over to his home in Weybridge. The two friends spent time discussing art and music and soon, Yoko began phoning John to talk to him. As their friendship grew, Yoko would turn up, sometimes unannounced, on John's doorstep. One time she got into the Rolls Royce with John and Cynthia and squeezed her way in-between the couple. When Cyn later asked John who she was, he told her she was just a weirdo wanting money for her "avant-garde bullshit". John did, in fact, financial support Yoko's next exhibition, Half A Wind, which opened in October 1967. Yoko next sent postcards to John almost daily and Cyn began to become suspicious of the couple's relationship.

Yoko wasn't the only women John had in his sights. John had wanted George's wife, Pattie Boyd, since he had set eyes on her back in 1964. At the launch party for Magical Mystery Tour, on 21 December 1967, a drunk John Lennon began flirting with Pattie in front of George and Cynthia. Another guest at the party, Scottish singer Lulu, marched over to John and told him "tend to your own wife before you make an even bigger fool of yourself". That seemed to do the trick as shortly afterwards he left with Cynthia in tow.

John and Yoko became so close that by February 1968, when The Beatles travelled to Rishikesh in India to study Transcendental Meditation under Maharishi Mahesh Yogi, John had to make the decision on who he should take along on the trip, Cynthia or Yoko. In the end he picked Cyn but he arranged for them to have separate beds. John spent many hours writing long letters to Yoko, who was waiting for him back in England. He wrote to her at least once a day and she wrote to him just as often. "I got so excited about her letters" John said later "There was nothing in them that wives or mothers-in-law could've understood. " It was during his time in India that John realised that he was in love with Yoko and he missed her. "From India I started thinking of her as a women, not just an intellectual woman" he said years later. He began writing songs about her, 'I'm So Tired', which would later appear on the 1968 album The Beatles (aka The White Album), was about Yoko. Other songs written at the time mentioned Yoko. She was 'Oceanchild' in 'Julia' (Yoko's name means oceanchild), the monkey in 'Everybody's Got Something to Hide Except Me and My Monkey' and later she was 'Mother Superior' in 'Happiness Is a Warm Gun' all of which would appear on the White Album. An unreleased song written by John during his time in India explains his feelings for Yoko at the time-"I left my heart in England with the girl I left behind."

As well as John and Cynthia Lennon, studying under the Maharishi at the same time were Paul McCartney and his girlfriend Jane Asher, Ringo Starr and his wife Maureen, George Harrison, his wife Pattie and her sister Jennie, folk singer Donovan, Mike Love of The Beach Boys, flautist Paul Horn, friend of The Beatles 'Magic' Alex Mardas, actress Mia Farrow and her sister Prudence (who John wrote 'Dear Prudence' for). At the time, Donovan was dating Jennie Boyd and had written 'Jennifer Juniper' for her shortly before the trip to India.

Ringo and Mureeen returned to England on 1 March with Paul and Jane Asher following on 26 March. Rumours began to spread across the camp that the Maharishi, despite claiming to be celibate, had had sexual relations with some of his young female students. According to Peter Brown, former assistant to Brian Epstein and now a board member of Apple Corps, a young blonde nurse from California had told him she had been wined and dined by the Maharishi in his private hut. Alex Mardas claims the same nurse told him she had had a sexual relationship with the Maharishi. Alex also claims that an American teacher called Rosalyn Bonas told both him and John Lennon that the Maharishi had made sexual advances towards her. Other accusations made about the Maharishi involved him making a pass at both Mia and Prudence Farrow as well as Jennie Boyd. George, Paul, Cynthia Lennon, and Jennie and Pattie Boyd have all said that the accusation were untrue but at the time John, George and Alex's minds were made up and on 12 April they packed their bags and left Maharishi's camp. When the Maharishi asked why they were leaving, John told him "If you're so cosmic, you'll know why". The Maharishi gave him a look as if he wanted to kill him.

The group booked taxis to take them to the airport but after they broke down several times they ended up hitchhiking to Delhi. On the way, John wrote a song he called 'Maharishi'. Back in England, he changed some of the lyrics and renamed it 'Sexy Sadie' and The Beatles recorded it for the White Album. Once on the plane, John began to drink, he hadn't drank since before coming to India and he quickly got very drunk. He'd already made up his mind that he was going to leave Cyn for Yoko and decided now was the perfect time to confess to the numerous affairs he had had since the couple had been together. One by one John reeled off names of women he had slept with included Alma Cogan,

Joan Baez and Cass Elliot.

Back in England, John couldn't wait to be with Yoko again. All he needed to do was get Cyn out of the way. In May, opportunity knocked when John heard that Donovan, his girlfriend Jennie Boyd, best friend 'Gypsy' Dave Mills, and 'Magic' Alex Mardas were planning a holiday in Greece and John suggested that Cyn went with them. She was reluctant at first and wanted John to join them but John insisted that he would be busy recording and that she should go without him, which is what she did, setting off on 6 May 1968. When she returned on 20 May she was in for a nasty shock but meanwhile John and Paul were in New York promoting The Beatles' new business Apple Corps.

During the four day trip Paul took some time off from interviews to spend time with Linda Eastman. After returning to England, John knew he only had a few days left before his wife returned and if he wanted to be alone with Yoko he would have to act fast. His main problem was nerves and he put off the meeting until the last minute. In the meantime, John sat at home, playing his guitar, writing songs, sleeping, and dropping acid with his best friend, Pete Shotton. One evening, he received a phone call from Derek Taylor-Brigitte Bardot was in London and wanted to meet The Beatles. John quickly agreed to meet her and Derek made the arrangements. John Lennon's fascination with the French actress was no secret, as a teenager he had her poster on his ceiling and he often masturbated over her. For John, she was the perfect woman and he was attracted to women who looked like her, including Pattie Boyd. He would fashion his girlfriends to look like Brigitte, buying them sexy outfits and convincing them to dye their hair blonde to better fit the role. John wasn't alone in this, Paul too had a thing for Brigitte and tried to transform his early girlfriend, Dot Rhone, into a Brigitte Bardot clone. For years, John's goal was to meet and seduce the French sex kitten. John first tried meeting her in 1964, when The Beatles came to Paris for the first time. Unfortunately, Brigitte was in Brazil at the time but her manager sent the boys a box of chocolates each with a card that read "Let's hope that these sweets will make up for her".

When Derek Taylor picked up John in a chauffeured car, he asked where the other Beatles were. Derek explained that Paul was in Scotland and George and Ringo had turned down the invitation to spend time with their wives. It would be only himself and John meeting Brigitte that night. John became nervous and suggested they dropped some acid before the meeting took place. Derek agreed, and they took acid in the back of the car on their way to Brigitte's hotel suite. As they arrived at the Mayfair Hotel, the acid began to kick in. Brigitte had had her room transformed into a Raj's palace with luxurious pillows on the floor to sit on. She had invited several gorgeous women to keep the group company and had made reservations at Parkes, a restaurant in Beauchamp Place. She had gone to great lengths to impress The Beatles but was disappointed when only John and Derek turned up.

John spoke very little French and Brigitte spoke no English, which made communication very difficult. As the night went on and the acid started to take full effect, Derek and John found themselves becoming more and more paranoid about leaving the hotel room. When it came to going out to the restaurant, John decided to stay behind and meditate. Brigitte quickly invited four other men to make up the numbers and left John and Derek in the hotel suite. When Brigitte and her guests returned to the suite, they were greeted by Indian music blasting out down the hall before they even made it back to the suite. Once inside her suite, Brigitte found John laid across the cushions surrounded by beer bottles. In her bedroom, she found Derek sprawled across her bed. She returned to the sitting room and tried to wake John up. After shaking him violently, he sat up, mumbled something, tried to sing to her, and then collapsed back into the cushions and went to sleep. John had come face to face with the woman of his dreams, he had been given the chance he had dreamed of since he was sixteen and not only had he blown it but he had blown it big time.

John eventually invited Yoko over on 19 May, a day before Cyn was due back. John already had a guest around, his friend Pete Shotton, when Yoko arrived. Unsure what to do with Yoko, he invited her to his basement and played her his private demo tapes.

"All this far-out stuff, some comedy stuff, and some electronic music" John remembered in 1970. Yoko was impressed and suggested they made one together. They spent the rest of the night recording what would later become the album Two Virgins. At dawn they made love for the first time. "It was very beautiful" John would later remember.

Yoko was still at the house when Cyn returned the next day. It was late afternoon when Cyn arrived at Kenwood with Jennie and Alex. At first, the house appeared to be empty, Cyn searched the rooms looking for any sign of life but she failed to find anyone. Where was her husband? Where was her son? Where was the housekeeper? Where was Pete Shotton? Cyn began to panic, something was terribly wrong. Eventually, in the Sun Room, she found John and Yoko sat on the floor, cross-legged and facing each other. John was dressed in his dressing gown while Yoko was wearing Cyn's bathrobe. When Cyn entered the room they greeted her like an old friend that had popped round. John looked at her and said "Oh, hi". Yoko didn't turn around. In shock at the situation, Cyn invited them to dinner which John turned down-Cyn turned and fled. She found Jennie and Alex in the kitchen and asked if she could stay with them in the house they shared. When they arrived at the house, Jennie immediately went to bed leaving Cyn and Alex to talk and drink red wine. As they were drinking their second bottle of wine, Alex told Cyn that he had always loved her and suggested they ran away together. Cyn got up to go to the bathroom and after being sick, she staggered towards a bedroom, where she passed out on the bed fully dressed. Sometime later, Alex got into bed with her and after waking her up, the couple began kissing. According to Peter Brown, Cyn and Alex slept together that night but Cyn denies these claims.

John wasn't the only one playing away from home. Paul had cheated on Jane Asher several times during their relationship. One of his secret lovers was Maggie McGivern, a dark haired model who was working as a nanny for Marianne Faithful and John Dunbar in 1966. Paul was friends with John Dunbar and would often visit him at his home in Chelsea. Maggie lived on the third floor of the flat and one day when Paul arrived unannounced, he buzzed the intercom to find out if John was in. Maggie answered and wanting to meet Paul she lied and said John was at home and let Paul in. Once Paul was in, Maggie confessed that John wasn't really at home and they both started laughing. The couple sat and ate lunch together and ended up chatting for hours. Paul would return to the flat more frequently asking to see Maggie. At first they were just friends, Paul was dating Jane Asher and Maggie was dating a photographer but both the relationships weren't going well and six months after their first meeting the pair became lovers.

One night, Paul brought along some demos of the Revolver album to play to John Dunbar and that night he slept with Maggie for the first time. "It was wonderful" Maggie remembered in 1997 "The next morning was one of the most precious moments of my life". Paul stayed at the flat with Maggie until lunchtime "we chatted and larked about" she remembers. The couple avoided being seen in public but managed to spend time together at Regents Park and the country side. In September 1966, Paul flew to Paris with Brian Epstein, on a separate flight was Maggie McGivern. It was important that Paul and Maggie were not spotted together by the press but once in Paris they could relax and met up. Paul, Brian and Maggie stayed in the same hotel and on the first day they met up with John Lennon and Neil Aspinall. John had been in Celle in West Germany filming How I Won The War and had come to Paris for the weekend during a break in filming. In Paris, the famous men were left alone, no one was expecting to see two Beatles walking the streets so they went almost unnoticed. They visited a flea market and the Eiffel Tower, where John and Paul laid under the tower and glazed up. Paul and Maggie continued to meet each other in secret for three years.

In 1967, Maggie stopped working for Marrianne Faithful and was running an antiques stall in Chelsea Market as well as continuing to model and had even had a part as an extra in the film Blow-Up. Maggie was busy living her life and it was always Paul who pursued her. "I hardly phoned him" she remembered in 1997. "He used to find me wherever I was and that was fine as far as I was concerned". In September 1967, Paul wanted Maggie to appear in The Beatles' TV film Magical Mystery Tour but couldn't find her in time to ask her. The couple had been together for over a year now and Maggie began to spend a lot of time at Paul's home in St John's Wood. "By this time I knew that I was in love with him, and I knew he loved me, too" said Maggie in 1997. In September 1968, Paul took Maggie on another holiday, this time he hired a private jet to take the couple to Sardinia. One day during the holiday, as the couple laid on the beach, Paul turned to Maggie and smiling he asked "Have you ever thought about getting married?" "Yes, I suppose, one day..." she replied. Looking back Maggie admits "It was obviously the wrong answer". The couple were photographed on the beach together and the photos were sold to a British newspaper and the relationship became public knowledge.

Not long after the couple returned to England, Paul became more involved with Linda and one day when Maggie rang Paul it was Linda who answered. Paul never officially ended the relationship but when he married Linda in March 1969 Maggie knew it was over. "I didn't contact him for ages" she said later. Maggie would bump into Paul a few times during the seventies and last saw her ex-lover in 1984.

Paul had also been romantically linked to The Beatles fan club secretary Frieda Kelly. Frieda had worked for the fan club since 1962 when she was seventeen and admits having a crush on each of The Beatles at one point or other. In 1967 she was photographed out and about with Paul McCartney and the next thing she knew, stories were appearing in the newspapers that Paul planned to marry her. The rumours were put to rest on 30 July when a statement was released denying the couple had wed.

Jane Asher never found out about Paul's relationship with Maggie McGivern but, Paul had a string of lovers and in July 1968 Jane would have an experiences similar to that of Cynthia Lennon in May of that same year. Jane had moved in with Paul and on Christmas Day 1967 the couple got engaged. In June 1968, Jane began a theatre tour while Paul began an affair with an American brunette called Francie Schwartz.

Fancie had arrived in England in 1968, looking for a buyer for the film script she had written and had ended up in the reception lounge of the Apple offices, where she met Paul for the first time. The pair chatted and Paul told her she could work in the Apple offices. She gave him her address and a few days later he turned up at her London home. The couple spent the afternoon together, having lunch and chatting. Paul sat with Francie on his lap and the couple kissed but they didn't take things any further. Later, Paul drove her to visit a friend in the country and they ran barefoot in the rain. Paul returned a week later on 8 June, after attending his brother, Michael's, wedding in North Wales. Again, Francie sat on Paul's lap and the couple sat chatting and kissing. "It's Fuck Day" Paul told her and the couple made their way upstairs where they made love for the first time. Francie became a regular visitor to Paul's house at Cavendish Avenue and claims that one day she found a letter to Paul from Brian Epstein. Francie claims the letter was a love letter begging for Paul to return his affection. If the claim is true, then Paul had held onto the letter for at least ten months as Brian had died in August 1967.

As far as Jane was concerned, Paul only had eyes for her and a year before, in an interview printed in the Daily Express, she was quoted as saying "I don't think either of us has looked at anyone else since we first met". The reality couldn't be any more different. In 1968, not only was Paul cheating on Jane with Francie Schwartz and Maggie McGivern but he was seeing Linda Eastman and Winona Williams. On 20 June, Paul flew to New York on a business trip and one of the first things he did on arriving in America was contact Linda Eastman and ask her to meet up with him in LA. The next day, Paul and his small entourage of Ron Kass, head of Apple Tony Bramwell and friend Ivan Vaughan, flew to Los Angeles, where they stayed at the Beverly Hills Hotel. Word got around that Paul McCartney was in town and that night "models and starlets were throwing themselves at us" remembers Tony and if they couldn't get hold of Paul they would have Ron, Tony or Ivan instead. "I think I ended up with an air-hostess" remembers Tony in his book Magical Mystery Tours "but it was hard to tell". According to Ron Kass, Paul ended up with African-American actress Winona Williams and a Swedish supermodel.

The next day, Paul finally got to meet up with Linda when she arrived at Paul's hotel. That night Paul took Linda to the Whiskey-A-Go-Go, where they watched B.B King and The Chicago Transit Authority perform. At the end of the night, Linda went back to the hotel with Paul and the couple made love. Linda would later refer to it as "a dirty weekend". The next day, as fans gathered outside the hotel, Paul and Linda stayed in bed making love. Eventually, Paul got out of bed and played 'Blackbird' to his fans waiting outside while Linda sat quietly in the background.

Famous musicians began turning up to the hotel wanting to see Paul including Roger McGuinn of The Byrds. Songwriters Tommy Boyce and Bobby Hart, who had written hits for The Monkees, telephoned and invited Paul to a toga party but Paul had told Tony Bramwell to turn down any invitations so he could spend all his time with Linda. The actress Peggy Lipton however couldn't take 'no' for an answer. She had been Paul's lover during The Beatles last two US tours in 1965 and 1966 and continued to ring the hotel all through the night. Paul and Linda spent the whole of the next day together. Warner Bros executive, John Calley, invited Paul and his entourage to sail on a yacht that he owned. Paul had to make a decision, if he took Linda on the trip their relationship would become public, if he didn't he would be wasting a day that he could be spending with Linda. In the end he decided to take her and if anyone was to ask, she was simply taking photos. When they left the hotel to get in the limo, Peggy Lipton turned up. She had come to spend the day with Paul but as soon as Paul saw her he told Tony "Oh my God, she can't come" and asked him to get rid of her. Tony told Peggy that it was strictly a private party and there was no way she could join them. Peggy became very upset and argumentative but the group drove off quickly, leaving her stood on the hotel steps in tears. Later that day, Paul and Linda returned to New York on separate flights and the next day, Paul returned to England, leaving Linda in New York.

Back in England, Paul continued his affair with Francie Schwartz. One day in mid-July, Jane Asher paid Paul and unexpected visit. Her theatre tour had ended early and she turned up at Cavendish Avenue to surprise Paul. Having her own key she let herself in, only to find her fiancée in bed with another woman. Francie was dressed in nothing but Paul's dressing gown-without saying a word Jane left. Later that evening, while Paul was recording in the studio, Jane's mother arrived at the house to collect some of Jane's belongings. Jane would officially announce the end of the relationship on 20 July, when she appeared the BBC program Dee Time. She announced the engagement was over telling the show's presenter, Simon Dee, "I haven't broken it off, but it is broken off, finished". Jane has never discussed her relationship with Paul in public since.

Paul continued to see Francie and for a few months she even moved in with him, doing the cooking, cleaning and entertaining house guests such as John and Yoko, who she adored. She also got to spend time with the group in the studio and remembers Paul playing 'Hey Jude' to her and telling her it was for her. Paul would later say that the song was in fact written for John's son, Julian, who was having a hard time after his parent's separation. The stress of recording could become too much for Paul at times and it was Francie who suffered Paul's darker side. During one stressful recording session Paul yelled "Juden Raus!" ("Jews, out!" in German) at his Jewish girlfriend. Francie left Paul in the late summer of 1968, when she returned to her parents' home in New Jersey.

Meanwhile, John's father, Alfred, had ended up working at the Toby Jug Hotel in Surrey. While there he met an eighteen-year-old girl called Pauline, a student working in the hotel during the holidays. The fifty-six-year-old Freddie and Pauline began seeing each other and soon fell in love. Pauline began working for John and Cynthia, helping Cyn out with housework and looking after Julian and she moved into Kenwood in October 1967. In early 1968, she moved out and moved in with Freddie in his flat in Kew. Pauline's mother was not happy with the relationship and applied to make her a ward of court. The press got hold of the story and the stress and tension caused two-month pregnant Pauline to suffer a miscarriage. Trying to move out of the public eye, Freddie and Pauline moved to a flat in Brighton, which John had bought for them. In June 1968, Pauline found herself pregnant again and

John paid for them to take a three-week holiday to Gretna Green in Scotland, where the couple got married. Their first son, David Henry, was born in February 1969 and John bought them a house in Brighton. They had another son, Robin in October 1973.

Alfred wasn't the only one starting a new life with a new family. Paul's father, Jim, married for the second time in November 1964. Jim, sixty-two at the time had first met his new wife-to-be Angela Lucia Williams, a few months earlier and had only met the thirty-four-year-old widow three times before marrying her. Angela, better known as Angie, had previously been married to Eddie Williams and had had a child, Ruth, with him in 1960. When Jim married Angie, the little girl was adopted by Jim and became Paul's legal step-sister. Ruth and Angie remember how fans would send fan mail to the McCartney family home in Liverpool despite Paul not living there. Among the normal fan mail, Ruth and Angie would open packages that contained used underwear and a notes that read 'Please give these to Paul'. Others would write and request used underwear belonging to Paul. This is only one example of weird behaviour displayed by fans that wanted to get close to their heroes. In 1968, a group of fans broke into Paul's flat in St John's Wood and helped themselves to many of Paul's personal items including his underwear. Paul did eventually manage to get the items back with the help of a group of fans called the Apple Scruffs. Paul's song about the incident, 'She Came in Through the Bathroom Window', would be released on The Beatles album Abbey Road.

9

The Ballad of Linda and Yoko

March 1969 saw two of the most famous men in the world marry women that were pretty much unknown by the fans and the public alike. Paul McCartney was the first to tie the knot, marrying Linda Eastman on 12 March. Before Marrying Paul, Linda had had up to twenty different lovers including rock stars Mick Jagger, Tim Buckley, and Jim Morrison, as well as actor Warren Beatty. She had been married once before to American geologist Joseph Melville See Jr., who she had met at the University of Arizona. The couple married in June 1962 and had a daughter together, Heather Louise in December that year. The marriage didn't last long and after their split in 1964, they divorced in June 1965. Linda had been one of Paul's regular groupies since 1967 and she moved in with him at the end of 1968. During those early days, the couple would drive off into the country together in Paul's car and purposely get lost. They would spend hours in the back of Paul's car fucking, and Linda found herself pregnant with Paul's child in January 1969. They quickly arranged a wedding at Marylebone Registry Office in London and shortly afterwards Paul adopted six-year-old Heather then, in August, Linda gave birth to a second daughter, Mary.

Most female fans reacted to Paul and Linda's marriage with tears-they wanted Paul for themselves and some thought Linda only wanted him for his money and fame but most fans accepted Linda. The same cannot be said of the marriage between John and Yoko a week later. John and Yoko's relationship had become public knowledge on 15 June 1968, when the couple planted acorns for peace in St Michael's Cathedral in Coventry. John filed for divorce the same month on the grounds of adultery, claiming Cyn had an affair with Magic Alex and Alex was willing to testify on John's behalf. Cyn failed for divorce herself in August on the grounds of John's adultery with Yoko. Both the public and the press hated Yoko Ono. The public saw her as a home wrecker-John was married and had a child and now he was leaving all that for Yoko. What was worse than that was Yoko herself. Yoko was Japanese and this was a big problem for the British public, who still considered Japan the enemy. It had been less than 25 years since the end of the Second World War and the British wanted nothing to do with Japan or the Japanese. Critics lashed out at John and Yoko and Yoko was attacked in the press. She was called ugly, a witch and a dragon lady. The general public were no better and Yoko couldn't leave the house without having abuse hurled at her. She received tons of hate mail and on occasion, she was physically attacked. Once, she even had a stone thrown at her head. Linda would suffer some abuse from fans but it was nothing compared to the abuse Yoko received. Things went from bad to worse for Yoko and it seemed everything she did made the public hate her more. Fans started to notice a change in John Lennon that they didn't like and they blamed Yoko. Then, in the morning of 18 October 1968, John and Yoko were busted for drug possession at the flat they were renting from Ringo at 34 Montagu Square in London. Small amounts of hashish and even smaller amounts of cannabis were found. John took the blame and was fined £150.

Things started to look up for the couple, when Yoko became pregnant and Cyn's divorce was granted on 8 November but, the happiness wasn't to last and on 21 November 1968, Yoko suffered a miscarriage. She had been admitted to Queen Charlotte's Maternity Hospital earlier in the month after fears that both the child and mother could lose their lives. Yoko had had at least one abortion in her past and the stress of the drug bust and the negative publicity meant that Yoko's chances of carrying the baby to full term were very slim. The baby boy, who was due in February 1969, was named John Ono Lennon II and was given a proper burial in a tiny casket. John was by Yoko's side throughout her time in hospital and slept on the floor in a sleeping bag after the bed he was using was needed by a patient. A newspaper report of the story was sung by Yoko and titled 'No Bed For Beatle John'. It was included on the couple's second album Unfinished Music No.2: Life With The Lions in

1969. The back cover also included a photo of Yoko in her hospital bed with John beside her in his sleeping bag. The album also included the baby's heartbeat, which was recorded by John and then repeated for five minutes. 'Baby's Heartbeat' was followed by 'Two Minutes Silence'. It was around this time that the couple started using heroin to help them cope with their emotional pain but Yoko would suffer a second miscarriage on 12 October 1969.

Once Yoko's divorce had been granted on 27 January 1969, the couple set about arranging their marriage. Originally, the couple wanted to get married in Paris but after that fell through they tried to get married on a ferry and then a cruise ship, hoping to arrive in France as a married couple but again that didn't go to plan. They next tried to get married in a British embassy but that required at least two weeks residence. Finally, on 20 March 1969, John and Yoko flew to Gibraltar where they were married at the British Consulate Office in a 10-minute ceremony.

Despite his own adultery, John was extremely jealous of any man who received Yoko's attention. He feared Yoko would leave him for another man and wanted to know who his competition was. Before marrying Yoko, John demanded she made a list of all the people she had slept with which included her first two husbands, Toshi Ichiyanagi and Tony Cox. The list also included all the men Yoko had cheated on her husbands with, that included the writer Michael Runmaker, violinist La Monte Young, painter Shusaku Arakawa, and John's bandmate Paul McCartney. John's jealousy often turned to violence and he hit Yoko on more than one occasion. One incident of such violence was immortalised in the song 'Jealous Guy'. After lashing out at Yoko one day in 1971, John needed a way to apologise and taking a tune he had written in 1968, he rewrote the lyrics and it became 'Jealous Guy'.

John and Yoko's honeymoon must be the most famous honeymoon in history with the couple taking to bed for a week in the Amsterdam Hilton Hotel between 25-31 March. The couple invited the world's press into their bedroom and rumours that the pair would be making love spread like wild fire but in fact, John and his new wife were dressed in pyjamas and talking about peace and love in their now famous 'Bed-in for Peace'.

However, there was plenty of other opportunities to see one or both members of the famous twosome in the nude. The most famous example being the front and back cover of their first album, Unfinished Music No.1: Two Virgins, which was released in November 1968. The front cover showed John and Yoko, completely naked, stood side by side with their arms around each other, while the back shows a similar shot but taken from the back. This time the couple are holding hands and looking over their shoulders. A third shot showing the couple holding a copy of The Time Business News over their genitals was not used.

The album cover was so controversial that it had to be covered with a brown paper bag when it went on sale. In America, some copies, including 30,000 copies in New Jersey, were impounded as obscene. Their third album, Wedding Album, was originally meant to come with a jigsaw puzzle of the cover photo of Two Virgins, but the piece with John's penis would fit were Yoko's vagina was and vice versa but EMI refused to approve the idea. One fan liked the Two Virgins photo so much that he photographed himself in the nude and using trick photography he made it appear he was stood next to the couple. He had the photo enlarged to poster size, framed and sent off to the Lennons. John liked it so much he hung it above his fireplace. When asked who the man was in 2000, Yoko replied she didn't know the man but referred to him as a professor.

John and Yoko's public nudity didn't stop there, shortly after the wedding, John drew a number of lithographs that became known as the Bag One Lithographs. The drawings showed scenes of the Lennon's wedding day and night including close up images of the couple preforming oral sex on each other. When the lithographs were exhibited at the Arts Gallery in New Bond Street, London, complaints were made and the police intervened. They seized some of the more erotic items under the Obscene Publications Act and removed them from the gallery. In August, the couple made a film together called Self-Portrait. The 42-minute-long movie focuses on John's penis showing it becoming erect in slow motion. The Lennons would continue to cause controversy throughout 1969 and the early seventies. The third verse of 'Give Peace a Chance' contains a reference to masturbation but, not wanting the song to be banned, it was changed to mastication on the official lyric sheet. Yoko's song 'Open Your Box' failed to avoid being banned when it was released in 1971 as the B-side to John's single 'Power to the People'. The song was banned in Britain because of its risky lyrics: 'Open your box, open your trousers, open your sex, open your legs' (Box is American slang for vagina). In America, Capitol Records refused to even issue the single and replaced the B-side with another Yoko Ono song-'Touch Me'. When the couple weren't appearing in the nude themselves they were paying others to strip off in the name of art and at the end of 1970 they began work on one of Yoko's films, Fly. The 50-minute film showed a fly crawling on the naked body of actress Virgina Lust.

In July 1983, soft-porn magazine Swank claimed they had found nude photos of John and Yoko in a dustbin and were going to publish them in their October issue. Yoko claimed the photos had been stolen from her and threatened to take legal action if they were published, but nude photos from the same session had already been published two years previously. In December 1979, Rolling Stone photographer, Annie Leibowitz, took several photos of John and Yoko in their apartment at the Dakota in New York. Some of the photos showed John and Yoko in the nude and one, showing a nude John clinging to a fully clothed Yoko, featured on the magazine's cover in January 1981. In 1971, John and Yoko gave an interview for the BBC Radio 2 programme Woman's Hour in which they discuss sex, love, and relationships. During the interview, Yoko declares "sex is like shaking hands" while John says "you can have sex without love". These two statements sum up the couples attitude towards sex and love.

In February 1969, The Beatles began recording sessions for would become their second to last album, Abbey Road. By now, John and Yoko were never apart and Yoko had sat in on her first Beatles' recording session in 1968. Before then, the group had had an unwritten rule that wives and girlfriends were not allowed in the studio. There were very few women in The Beatles' entourage. As James Brown had sang in 1966, it was a man's world. Now here was Yoko Ono turning up to every session with John. Not only that but Yoko wasn't happy to sit quietly in the corner and watch the band play, she wanted to get stuck in and she did just that. She would suggest ideas and even jam with the band. She added her vocals to 'The Continuing Story of Bungalow Bill', 'Revolution 9' and 'Birthday' on the White Album as well as the outtake 'What's The New Mary Jane' from that album. Outtakes from The Beatles next album, Let It Be, recorded in January

1969, include jam sessions that involved Yoko.

During the recording of Abbey Road, John and Yoko took their children, Julian and Kyoko, on a holiday to Scotland. John had never been the best driver and on 1 July he drove his car into a ditch. All four passengers were taken to Golspie's Lawson Memorial Hospital, where John was given 17 stitches, Yoko 14, and Kyoko four. Julian was unharmed. Once he returned to the sessions, John had a king-size bed installed into the studio so that Yoko, who had injured her back in the crash, could join him. John loved the idea of Yoko being in the studio and even suggested that the group should expand and include Yoko, Eric Clapton and Billy Preston among others. Eric had played on a few Beatle sessions before and Billy was involved heavily in the recording of Let It Be. The other three, especially George and Paul, couldn't stand Yoko and didn't want her in the studio let alone the band. It's no wonder that John thought 'Get Back' had originally been written about his new wife.

Yoko's constant presence in the studio has been said to have been one of the key factors in the break-up of the band but when fans were interviewed in 1970 it was Linda who got all the blame not Yoko and in 2013, Paul went on record to say Yoko was not to blame for the group's split. It would take a lot more than one woman to break-up The Beatles and like Pete's sacking in 1962, a number of things contributed to the break-up of The Beatles, not just Yoko Ono.

One evening, before a session for Abbey Road, John turned up at Paul's house at Cavendish Avenue unannounced to check with Paul what time that day's session was taking place. When he arrived he found Linda was home alone. She let John in but informed him that Paul had already left for the studio. They began talking and shared a bottle of wine. Once all the wine was gone Linda rolled a giant joint that they proceeded to smoke. Linda excused herself and returned to the bedroom, where she had been making the bed before John had turned up. John followed her and offered her a hand. As they made the bed, John's arm brushed against Linda and they kissed. The famous groupie couldn't resist the famous Beatle despite being married to his bandmate. After all it was John she had first set her sights on. Drunk and high, they fell into each other's arms and made love on Paul's bed.

In April 1970, The Beatles went their separate ways. There are many reasons why the group split, so many in fact you could write a book about it and most likely someone already has. The Beatles had grown up, ten years ago they were four young lads from Liverpool that hadn't experienced much in the way of sex and drugs, now they were married men of the world. They had experimented in drugs, religious beliefs, and sex and now they were ready to kick the groupies out and settle down. That is all but one member of the group, the youngest group member, George Harrison. Despite being married to

Pattie Boyd since 1966, George was not ready to stick to one woman just yet. George had always had a special relationship with a group of fans called the Apple Scruffs, who would hang outside Abbey Road studios and The Beatles' homes. He even wrote a song for them called 'Apple Scruffs' for his 1970 album All Things Must Pass. One day, in 1972, he turned up on the doorstep of the bedsit of one of the Apple Scruffs. Carol Bedford was originally from Texas and had moved to London to be closer to The Beatles. She remembers how George turned up uninvited and rang the doorbell to her bedsit. When Carol answered George stepped inside, closing the door behind him. He threw his arms around her and they began kissing for several minutes. Carol claims that they only kissed but for George this was more than a passing fling. His marriage to Pattie hadn't been going too smoothly and George wanted a divorce. He wanted to see other women and Carol was on his list. Of course he couldn't carry out his affair in London under the noses of Pattie and the press and a few days after the encounter he came up with a plan. Carol could move to Los Angeles, George had an apartment there that she could stay in and George could date her there without being spotted by the media. George sent Mal Evans to Carol's London bedsit to tell her the plan but Carol turned down the offer and was so upset by the idea that George would cheat on Pattie that she ceased being an Apple Scruff then and there.

Meanwhile, Paul and Linda had moved to Scotland and started to start their own family. Their second daughter together, Stella Nina McCartney, was born 13 September 1971. Paul had formed a new group called Wings, which he had taken on the road playing at universities across Britain in February 1972. The tour was followed by a European tour in the summer of the same year. During the tour, guitarist Denny Laine first met the women who would later become his wife. Nineteen-year-old Joanne LaPatrie (known as Jo Jo) was an American model and a well-known groupie. She had lost her virginity at Woodstock in 1969 to Jimi Hendrix. She next slept with Jim Morrison of The Doors before starting a two year relationship with Rod Stewart, who wrote 'You Wear It Well' about her. After leaving Rod she set her sights on Paul McCartney who she'd had a crush on since her early teens. Jo Jo had sent endless fan letters to Paul when he was in The Beatles. "She was basically trying to go through me to get to Paul" Denny later admitted. Jo Jo's biggest problem was that Paul was married and his wife, an active member of Wings, was on the road with him. Nothing got past Linda's watchful eye and she was suspicious of Jo Jo from day one. Jo Jo finally settled for Denny who she later married and had two children with. Jo Jo would eventually bed a Beatle, just not Paul.

10

Wife Swap

George Harrison was becoming well known for his affairs, he was sleeping with everyone from groupies to employees. His marriage to Pattie Boyd was no secret but very few women would turn down the chance to sleep with an ex-Beatle. One woman who did rebuff his sexual advances was Apple employee Chris O'Dell. Chris started working for Apple in 1968 and had been employed by George shortly after he bought Friar Park in Henley. Chris became George's assent and moved in to Friar Park. George spent a lot of time around Chris and it was obvious he was attracted to her. He became obsessed by Chris, while Pattie became suspicious of the couple's relationship and was convinced that George had only employed Chris so he could sleep with her. Despite her suspicions, Pattie befriended Chris during her time at Friar Park but, one night, she made the condition of their friendship very clear. She told Chris, in no uncertain terms, that they would remain friends as long as she didn't let George 'have' her. Chris agreed but she remembers George as being "a very flirtatious man" and admits that he made a few passes but she would always reject him. Instead of sleeping together, Chris claims they would stay up talking into the early hours, long after everyone else had gone to bed.

After being fired from Apple, Chris O'Dell worked for Eric Clapton for a while before moving to Los Angeles to work for Peter Asher in 1971. A few months after moving to L.A, Chris got a phone call from her ex-employee and friend, George Harrison. George was in L.A on a business trip and wanted to know if Chris wanted to keep him company. It was getting late so, Chris promised George she would call him the next day and arrange a visit but she never did. Days went by and George still hadn't received a phone call from her. Picking up his guitar he began to compose: "Why won't you call me Miss O'Dell" and then he called her. Eventually, George got his wish and Chris spent a day with him at the house he was renting in Los Angeles. He played her the song he had written about her. The song, 'Miss O'Dell', would later become the B-side to his 1973 single 'Give Me Love (Give Me Peace On Earth)'. It wasn't the first time Chris had been captured in song, her ex-boyfriend, Leon Russell, had written 'Pisces Apple Lady' and 'Hummingbird' for her.

Chris O'Dell remembers the moment George Harrison told her he was in love with Ringo's wife, Maureen. It was the morning of 23 December 1973 and Chris was spending Christmas with the Harrisons at Friar Park and that morning George arrived at Chris' room bringing her a cup of tea. As he sat on the edge of the bed the two chatted away. Then, as if out of nowhere, he told her "You know I'm in love with Maureen." Stunned, Chris looked up from her cup of tea, "Wow" she said. "That's all I could manage" she remembered later "I just stared at him." The night before Chris had noticed some odd goings on in Friar Park. That night the Harrisons had had two guests round, Maureen Cox and Ronnie Wood, who at the time was a member of The Faces but would later join The Rolling Stones. That night, the group separated into two, Ronnie and Pattie sat in the library, chatting and giggling, while George and Maureen sat in the Main Hall, deep in conversation leaving Chris to flutter between the two rooms. For George this was usual behaviour-Maureen had become a regular visitor to Friar Park, often staying the night. George and Maureen would spend the night together alone, some nights they would lock themselves into a room and when Pattie would go looking for her husband, she would find him locked in a room with another women. Pattie was ignored by the couple and when they did answer her it was to tell her to leave them alone.

It was Christmas Eve 1973 when everything came out in the open. Maureen rang Friar Park and George answered, but it was Chris she wanted. She invited her to spend the evening with herself and Ringo at Tittenhurst. The Starkeys had bought the house from the Lennons in August 1971, when the latter moved to America. When Chris told Pattie and George her plans for the night, George told her he would go too, saying he'd like to see Ringo. Knowing it wasn't Ringo that George wanted to see but Maureen, Pattie insisted on going as well. As Ringo, George, Pattie, and Chris sat around the kitchen table, Maureen kept herself busy refilling drinks and cooking food. At one point in the night, Maureen pulled out a packet of Marlboros cigarettes from a drawer. Only George smoked Marlboros, the Starkeys smoked Larks. She placed the cigarettes next to George who looked up and gave her a smile. The room fell into silence. As Maureen cleared the table, George spurted out his secret just as he had to Chris the day before, "You know, Ringo, I'm in love with your wife". Again the room went into absolute silence. Similar words would come back to haunt George later when Eric Clapton would confess his love for Pattie. Ringo looked down at the table, flicked his cigarette ash into the ashtray and said nothing. After what seemed like an age of silence, Ringo looked up "Better you than someone we don't know" he said. Chris turned to Pattie "let's go into the other room" she suggested and the two friends left. George then suggested that they swapped wives for the rest of the evening. Ringo stormed off, the angriest he'd been in a long time. An embarrassed Maureen left to find Pattie and Chris. Pattie held no grudge against Maureen and the three women chatted like nothing had happened.

George and Maureen's affair continued for a few more weeks. One evening when Pattie returned home from a day of shopping, she found George in bed with Maureen. When he was later asked about the incident George shrugged his shoulders and said "Incest, I guess".

George liked the idea of a wife swap and when during a party at his home, Friar Park, in 1973, Ronnie Wood of The Faces told George he was going to sleep with Pattie that night he was fine with the idea. He told Ronnie that he would sleep with his wife, Krissie instead. When it came to going to bed the two men stood on the landing outside the bedrooms. "Are we going to do this?" Ronnie asked to which George joked "I'll see you in court" before going into the bedroom where Krissie was. That night George slept with Ronnie's wife while Ronnie slept with Pattie and in the morning George joked that he had already called his lawyers. A few weeks later, George took Krissie on a holiday to Portugal and then Switzerland to meet Salvador Dali, leaving Pattie and Ronnie behind.

Krissie Wood, born Kissie Findlay in 1948, had dated a number of musicians since her teens. She lost her virginity to Eric Clapton in 1963 when he was in The Yardbirds. She then dated Ronnie Wood of The Small Faces and they married in 1971. He wrote 'Mystifies Me' and 'Breathe On Me' for her. She began her affair with George Harrison in 1973 while Pattie and Ronnie began an affair and the pair holidayed together in the Bahamas. Krissie is also rumoured to have had slept with John Lennon in 1973. After leaving George she flew to Los Angeles where she met up with John. She spent time with him in the studio and they were seen at parties together. Krissie left John to be reunited with Ronnie in New York. There she met Jimmy Page and began her next affair. She eventually returned to Ronnie and they had a son, Jesse, together in 1977. By then, however, Ronnie had met Jo Howard, who became his second wife.

Meanwhile, Ringo had his sights set on Chris O'Dell and in February 1974, he flew to L.A to be with her. After the drama on Christmas Eve, Maureen had suggested to Chris that maybe she should be with Ringo. Chris thought she was joking and laughed it off but now she was calling Chris in L.A asking her to look after her husband. Ringo arrived on Valentine's Day and meet up with Chris later that night at the after party for a Bob Dylan concert. A few days later Ringo invited Chris to a party being held at the Beverly Wilshire by record producer David Geffen. After the party the couple ended up at Ringo's hotel room, drinking and talking late into the night. It was five in the morning before Ringo went to bed and Chris drove her car to work, where she slept until the office opened.

Ringo returned to England later that week but only six weeks would pass before he came back to L.A. Ringo phoned Chris the day after he arrived and invited her to the Record Plant, where John Lennon and Mick Jagger were working on 'Too Many Cooks (Spoil the Soup)'. John was with May Pang (more on that later) and as the men worked on the track the two women got talking, finding themselves in similar situations. As the song was played back,

Ringo took Chris by the hand and danced with her across the studio. That night Chris wrote in her diary "We danced. R & I definitely were feeling attracted to each other."

After the session, the two couples found themselves at a party being held by film director Roman Polanski. Ringo and Chris spent hours drinking, talking and holding hands and when Ringo returned to the Beverly Wilshire that night with John and May he had Chris by his side. They spent many more hours on the balcony looking out on the Beverly Hills skyline. Without saying goodnight Ringo took himself off to bed. Chris wondered if she should join him but eventually left. Ringo rang her the next morning and invited her to lunch at Roger Moore's house. Things became awkward when Luisa Moore asked about Maureen on more than one occasion. After lunch, Ringo quickly made an excuse and the couple left for the Beverly Wilshire. "That was fun" Ringo said as they drove back to the hotel, "Let's not do it again."

Chris and Ringo's affair began there and then and Chris spent the next three weeks with Ringo. Ringo eventually moved into the beach house in Santa Monica that John had rented from Peter Lawford. President Kennedy once was a frequent visitor at the mansion while having his affair with actress Marilyn Monroe, so it was the ideal setting for the two married ex-Beatles to set up home with their lovers.

The affair ended in June, when Maureen turned up in L.A and straight up asked Chris, "Are you sleeping with my husband?" Maureen had rung Chris about a week earlier after hearing rumours of Ringo's new girlfriend, and had asked her if she knew who it was. Chris lied saying she hadn't even heard the rumours. A week later, Maureen arrived in Los Angeles to find out for herself. Chris avoided her calls for days but it was no good, Maureen was determined and when she finally got through to Chris, Maureen invited her over for dinner. It was during that dinner that Maureen confronted her husband and his lover. Chris knew something like this was going to happen and had planned to deny it all and had informed Ringo to do the same but, when push came to shove, she admitted it all. "Well, at least you were honest with me" Maureen said.

George's next affair would begin the same year, when he began dating actress Kathy Simmonds. The twenty-four-year-old had starred in the 1968 film The Touchables and had dated Rod Stewart and Harry Nilsson. The couple moved in together in a villa near St George's Bay in Grenada. They spent several weeks there before George moved to Los Angeles to plan his first solo tour leaving Kathy behind. Meanwhile, Pattie had left George to be with Eric Clapton, who she had been having an affair with. Eric and Pattie first met in 1968, while Eric was working with George and The Beatles. Eric and George became close friends and they spent a lot of time together. George had even written the song 'Savoy Truffle' about Eric's love of chocolate. It wasn't long before Eric fell in love with Pattie and in 1970, he wrote the songs 'Layla' and 'Bell Bottom Blues' about her. Eric started dating Pattie's younger sister, Paula, and they moved in together. She later left him after hearing 'Layla', and realising that Eric was in love with her sister. Pattie rebuffed Eric's advances until 1974 when she left George to begin her affair with him. Eric hadn't been the only one that had tried to seduce Pattie, Mick Jagger had tried too for years but had failed every time. It's hard to say what actually happened between Eric and Pattie in the early stages of their relationship, Eric's autobiography says one thing while Pattie's says another. One thing that is known is that one night Eric confessed his love for Pattie and told George "I have to tell you, man, I'm in love with your wife." George had heard it all before. Gerry Marsden had used similar words in 1961 and George had told Ringo he was in love with Maureen a few years before and now it was George's turn again. Maybe karma is real after all.

George couldn't really grumble, he'd already slept with one of Eric's ex-girlfriends. Eric and Charlotte Martin had been dating since 1967 but in December 1968 the couple had an argument and Eric kicked the French model out. Eric then began dating the daughter of Lord Herlech, Alice Ormsby-Gore and they became engaged in September 1969 but never married. Meanwhile,

Charlotte moved into the Harrison's home, Knifauns, in December 1968 and began an affair with George. It was on New Year's Day 1969 that Pattie became suspicious but George told her she was just being paranoid. Pattie left George and moved to London for six days. Eventually, George ended the affair and phoned his wife telling her Charlotte had left and asked her to come home.

Pattie and George divorced in June 1977 and Pattie moved in with Eric. That year Eric wrote 'Wonderful Tonight' about Pattie and they married on 27 March 1979 in Tucson, Arizona. The official wedding celebration wasn't held until after Eric's Backless tour ended. A party was held at the Claptons' home, Hurtwood Edge and the guests included George Harrison, Paul McCartney and Ringo Starr, and all three ex-Beatles jammed on stage.

Ringo's marriage was falling apart too. Ringo would later describe himself as "a drunk, a wife-beater and an absent father". He had been having an affair with American model Nancy Lee Andrews which lead to the Starkey's divorce in July 1975. Depressed over the end of her marriage, Maureen attempted to take her own life by driving a motorbike into a brick wall. She recovered and in 1989 she married Isacc Tigrett, who she'd met in 1976. Isacc, who was known for collecting memorabilia and was one of the founders of Hard Rock Cafe, had once called Maureen his "Ultimate collectible". The couple had a daughter together, Augusta King Tigrett, who was born 4 January 1987.

Sadly, Maureen died of leukaemia in 1994, at the age of 48. Ringo was by her side when she passed away and Paul wrote the song 'Little Willow' in her memory which was later released on his 1997 album Flaming Pie.

Ringo was marry for a second time in 1981, when he married actress Barbara Bach. In-between his two marriages, Ringo had a number of lovers but his main girlfriend was model Nancy Lee Andrews. Six years younger than Ringo, Nancy had been dating Ringo since 1974, when he was still married to Maureen. Nancy had moved in with Chris O'Dell when she broke up with Carl Radle. At the time, Chris was having an affair with Ringo but, when Maureen found out, Ringo called it off but it wasn't long before Chris was replaced by Nancy. When asked about the affair Nancy was to say "I am not a marriage wrecker. I'd hate to be thought of as a marriage wrecker. Everything between Ringo and Maureen was finished a year and a half before we met". In January 1975, Ringo took his new girlfriend on a holiday to London where he showed her around the sites before returning to California on 7 February. The couple moved to Monte Carlo in December 1975 for tax reasons but returned to England to spend Christmas at Tittenhurst Park.

Ringo and Nancy's relationship was on and off throughout the seventies, and during a break from her, Ringo began to date singer Lynsey De Paul. Lynsey, ten years Ringo's junior, was first spotted by Ringo's side at the premiere of The Man Who

Would Be King at the Odeon Theatre in London in December 1975. The singer-songwriter would write a song about her lover called 'If I Don't Get You (The Next One Will)', which she released as a single in April 1976, but by then Ringo had left her and returned to Nancy Lee Andrews. Ringo was in love with Nancy and proposed to her. Nancy said 'yes' and remembers "I wanted to settle down with him and raise a family". Ringo kept putting the wedding date off and in the meantime the couple wrote the song 'Las Brisas' together with was released on Ringo's 1976 album Ringo's Rotogravure. Ringo and Nancy's relationship wasn't perfect and during the mid-Seventies Ringo was also spotted around town with Susan Alpert, who he took on a date to a restaurant in Los Angeles. Actress Debralee Scott, who had starred in American Graffiti, was also dating Ringo for a while as was actress Shelley Duvell. Born on Ringo's ninth birthday, Shelley would later go on to date Paul Simon for three years. During one of his breaks from Nancy, in 1979, Ringo met nineteen-year-old Stephanie La Motta. Born in 1960, Stephanie was a massive twenty years younger than Ringo when she met him in the London nightclub Tramp in October 1979. The couple got talking and as they held hands under the table Ringo asked the young girl if she wanted to go to Vienna with him the next day. Shocked and not knowing what to do, Stephanie asked for more time to think about the proposal. Ringo took her to a disco in Mayfair but, unfortunately the doorman was just about to lock up. Not wanting to miss out on another hour of dancing, Ringo paid the doorman £100 to open up the disco for an extra hour. According to Stepanie, Ringo's ex-wife Maureen turned up and asked "Who is this, Ringo, the next Mrs. Starkey?" to which Ringo replied "Maybe Maureen, but be sure you'll be the first to know". Ringo then asked Stephanie about Vienna again and this time she agreed. Stephanie packed her bags and returned with Ringo to the Dorchester Hotel.

The couple shared a bed that night but didn't sleep together. Instead, Stephanie was asleep as soon as her head hit the pillow. The next day, they flew to Vienna, where they checked in to the Bristol Hotel. At the hotel they shared a king-size bed and slept together for the first time. "It surprised Ringo that I was so inexperienced" Stephanie remembers "I think he was pleased I hadn't slept with many men". The couple spent four days in Vienna, with Ringo taking his new lover to restaurants and bars in-between seeing the sights. The couple became closer as the days went on and soon found themselves falling in love. "We danced down the street singing 'Singing In The Rain'" Stephanie remembers. On the third day they were joined by Ringo's friend and fellow musician, Harry Nilsson. That night, the trio visited one of the city's clubs where Harry got on stage and sang the 20s pop standard 'Always'. While Harry sang, Ringo and Stephanie danced, Ringo pulled Stephanie closer and whispered "Darlin, I'm falling in love with you".

Stephanie told him that she was falling for him too. The couple were happy together and enjoying their time in the city, Stephanie remembers on their last day in Vienna "Ringo grabbed me in his arms and waltzed me round and round one of the city squares as Harry hummed a Strauss waltz". The next day, the couple flew to Greece to continue their holiday. After spending the weekend in Greece, Ringo was due to return to Monte Carlo and Stephanie was going to return to London and then New York. Not wanting to be parted, Ringo flew to London with Stephanie, but the romance wasn't to last and once back in London the couple saw very little of each other and when Stephanie flew to New York the affair ended.

Another of Ringo's girlfriends from 1979 was the model Samantha Juste. Born Sandra Slater in Manchester, England in 1944 she became a model in her teens and changed her name to Samantha Juste. She first met Ringo in 1968 while she was dating Micky Dolenz of The Monkees. She is "the being known as Wonder Girl" in the song 'Randy Scouse Git' and she married Micky Dolenz in 1968. They had a daughter, Ami Bluebell Dolenz, together in 1969. They divorced in 1975. Samantha remained friends with Ringo throughout the seventies and they began dating in 1979.

11

Another Girl

John and Paul's marriages were also hitting rocky patches. While Paul and Linda had moved to Scotland and were beginning their new family, John and Yoko had moved to New York to the revolutionary front line. The couple quickly made friends with radicals like David Peel, Jerry Rubin, and Abbie Hoffman. During a party at Jerry's apartment on election night 1972, John drank more than his fair share of beer and got very drunk. He began flirting with a woman at the party and asked her if she'd like to "fuck a Beatle", while Yoko looked on, tears in her eyes. He then began to fondle the woman's breasts before taking her into a bedroom and making love to her. The rest of the guests, including Yoko, could hear John and his lover through the walls and one guest kindly turned the volume up on the television set to drown out the noise for a now sobbing Yoko. Yoko would later write the song 'Death of Samantha' about the incident, which she released on her 1973 album Approximately Infinite Universe. When asked about the night in question, Yoko would say "Something was lost that night for me".

The Lennons' marriage would take a bigger blow in 1973, when the couple broke up for 18 months.

During the separation John would begin his now-famous affair with May Pang.

Ten years younger than John, May Pang was born to Chinese parents living in Spanish Harlem in 1950. She was hired by ABKCO records in 1970, but after 16 months she left and became the Lennons' personal assistant. The Lennons' love life had hit a rocky patch after the election night situation and May was approached by Yoko Ono in August 1973. Yoko knew that if she separated from her husband he would start seeing other women and suggested to May that she should become John's regular partner. At least that way she'd know who John was sharing his bed with. She told May, "John and I are not getting along. We've been arguing. We're growing apart. John will probably start going out with other people. May, I know he likes you." May protested at first but Yoko insisted and told her that John had already admitted to finding her attractive and ensured her that she would arrange everything. May knew it wasn't a suggestion but an order.

May's only previous sexual experience had been a love affair with Mike Gibbins, the drummer with Badfinger. Yoko told May that she should begin the affair that night during the Mind Games session but John cancelled the session and instead the affair began the following night. That night, when May and John left the Dakota for the session, John grabbed May in the elevator and began kissing her. "I've been wanting to do this all fuckin' day" he told her as she backed away in shock. For three nights in a row, John tried to take May home with him after that night's session. She refused to have an affair with her boss and for two nights she turned him down. On the third night John cancelled the limousine and instead took May back to her flat in a cab. The cab dropped them off outside May's flat and the couple began kissing. John pleaded to be let into the flat and once inside he made his advance. That night May Pang and John Lennon slept together for the first time. They then made love every night for the next two weeks.

In September 1973, Yoko left New York and flew to Chicago to attend a feminist congress. John and May took this opportunity to move out to Los Angeles. Originally, the couple were staying at Lou Adler's mansion but would later rent a beach house in Santa Monica. While living in L.A., John would enjoy a very active social life, hanging out with the likes of Harry Nilsson, Keith Moon, and Ringo Starr, all of whom were known for their heavy drinking habits. John began drinking heavily and snorting cocaine. Under the influence of drink and drugs, John would become violent towards May. He would often strangle her and once he even threw her across the room and into a wall. John also had a very loving side and he wrote the song 'Surprise, Surprise (Sweet Bird of Paradox)' for her. The song later appeared on the 1974 album Walls and Bridges.

One wild night at the Troubadour Club would end

with John on the front page of the papers the next day, after he was kicked out of the club. One night, a blind drunk John had to be tied to the bed for his own and other's safety, while another night he wrecked Harold Seider's apartment while out of his mind on vodka. That night ended with John wrestling with Jesse Ed Davis on the living room floor before John tried kissing the guitarist, which resulted in Jesse biting John's tongue. It was the second time that John had tried to kiss Jesse Ed Davis. The first time John had tried it, Jesse had kissed him back, which resulted in John pushing him away and calling him a 'faggot'.

During the Lost Weekend, as John later called it, John took the opportunity to meet up with some old friends including Ringo Starr, Paul McCartney, and The Beatles' former roadie Mal Evans. Mal had worked with The Beatles throughout the sixties and was now living in Los Angeles, where he was working on a book called Living The Beatles Legend. Mal's wife, Lily, had left him in 1973. They had been married since 1961, when Mal was 26. They had had two children together, Gary and Julie, in the sixties but now the two Liverpudlians had gone their separate ways and Mal was living with his new girlfriend, Fran Hughes. Once John found out Lily had left Mal, he wasted no time in finding out her whereabouts and sleeping with her. The guilt of sleeping with his friend's wife would haunt him after Mal was shot dead by police in 1976, at the age of 40. A depressed Mal Evans, high on

Valium at the time, had locked himself inside a room with an unloaded 30-30 rifle. When police turned up on the scene, he refused to put the gun down and they fired six shots, four of them hit the target and Mal died instantly.

John and May's affair became known to the public on 13 March 1974, when they were photographed together at the Troubadour Club. When John spotted the photographer he grabbed May by the neck and pulled her in for a kiss. The couple were snapped and the photo appeared in the papers the next day. Meanwhile, Yoko Ono was having an affair with David Spinozza. One night, when John was spotted out without Yoko, someone asked "Where's Ono?" to which John snapped "Sucking Ringo's dick!" The Lost Weekend was arguably John's most productive period and it saw him working on a number of projects including producing Harry Nilsson's album Pussy Cats but the constant drugs, drink, and parting was slowing down the progress and a frustrated John moved back to New York to finish the editing of the album away from Harry Nillson and the rest of the band.

Harry followed John to New York with his girlfriend, Lil, in tow. One night in New York, Harry took John to a brothel but John left saying he wasn't interested in fucking whores and instead returned to the house he was sharing with Harry and Lil. Back at the house, he found Lil alone and informed her what had happened. The two had shared a night of passion together before in Palm Beach, so when

John asked Lil to sleep with him again that night she had no objections. Besides, her boyfriend was out having his way with a bunch of prostitutes. "He didn't seem to be interested in the fucking part, although we did that" Lil reviled later "he wanted to be held basically." "I don't even recall that he came" she added. When Harry returned, nothing was said about what had happened but he soon found out when both John and himself discovered they had crabs and John had to admit to sleeping with Lil.

Another night in New York, John visited a bar called Jim Day's where he staggered around drunkenly telling every woman in sight "I'm John Lennon. Suck my cock". Unsurprisingly, no one took him up on it. That night he was joined by a fan by the name of Tony Manero, who claims John come on to him asking if he was gay (to which he replied 'no man, I don't go that way') and asking him for a blowjob. Later that night, when they left the bar, John put his arm around Tony telling him, "There's nothing wrong in being gay" and asking if he'd ever tried gay sex. Tony said he hadn't. John told him, "it feels good to hold someone". The Lennon party made their way to the Pierree Hotel, where John and Harry Nilsson had been staying. Once in the hotel room, John fancied his chances with Tony once again and putting his arm around him he tried to fondly and kiss him before Tony told him to stop. That night they slept in separate rooms. "After he died I wished I'd done it" Tony told a New York magazine. John later explained his actions in March 1975. Although he didn't mention this specific gay encounter he told NME reporter Lisa Robinson, "I was trying to put it around that I was gay, you know. I thought that would throw them off. Dancing at all the gay clubs in Los Angeles, flirting with the boys...but it never got off the ground". This seems unlikely, if John wanted the press to think he was gay all he had to do was tell them he was. What's more likely is that John was enjoying himself "playing it a bit faggy".

On 14 November 1974, the off-Broadway musical, Sgt. Pepper's Lonely Hearts Club Band on the Road, opened at the Beacon Theatre in New York and among the audience was John Lennon and May Pang. An after party was held at the Hippopotamus disco, which John and May attended. At the party, John made a move on a number of women including Ronnie Spector and Mick Jagger's wife Bianca. Both women turned him down but he was photographed kissing actress Alaina Reed Hall. She had the part of Lucy in the musical but was best known as Olivia in the children's television show Sesame Street. When it came to leaving time it wasn't Alaina that John left with but international model Donyale Luna and her friend. John left May to make her own way home. John had first met Donyale in December 1968, when she appeared on The Rolling Stones Rock n Roll Circus. John, along with photographer Bob Gruen made their way to Donyale's apartment where they were spotted by the press. After a failed attempt to get the two women to sleep together, John took Donyale into one of the bedrooms and did the job himself. After sleeping with Donyale, a pissed John staggered into the living room and, after not being able to find a song he liked playing on any of the radio stations, proceeded to smash the model's beat box by throwing it across the room. He then left for another model's house.

During the separation, Yoko would call John daily and would have her friends spy on him. She wanted to know her husband's every move-What he was doing and who. By the autumn of 1974, John had grown closer to May and was moving away from Yoko. He began refusing to take Yoko's calls and would slam the phone down mid-conversation. Yoko would threaten divorce but instead of breaking down and begging Yoko to take him back, John snapped at her telling her to hurry up and "get it over with". John was planning to buy a house with May and leave Yoko for good. His actions mirrored those of the late sixties when he had left Cynthia for Yoko but all this was about to change when, in January 1975, Yoko asked John to come back and, with his tail firmly between his legs, he returned to Yoko and the Dakota but not before sleeping with May one last time. John told May that Yoko had given him permission to keep a mistress but that's not what May wanted and their relationship ended there and then.

Suspicious of the sudden change, May suspects

fowl play and believes Yoko may have used brainwashing techniques and hypnotherapy to get her husband back. May also believes that a Beatles reunion may have taken place if John hadn't got back with Yoko. Jealous of May, for many years Yoko tried to delete her from history. On the song '#9 Dream' it's May you hear whispering John's name but years later, when putting together a music video for the song, Yoko filmed herself mouthing May's vocals.

The Lennons' sex life, which had dried up before the separation, was restored and on the night of 7 February 1975 Yoko conceived a baby boy. The Lennons had had problems when it came to Yoko becoming pregnant. Yoko had suffered two miscarriages during the late sixties and because of his heavy drug use, John had a low sperm count. So, when Yoko found herself pregnant, the couple saw it as somewhat of a miracle. During Yoko's pregnancy the doctors forbid sexual intercourse and John would satisfy his sexual urges by visiting Manhattan brothels. One of those brothels was a Korean house on 23rd street where John could enjoy sexual encounters either on a one to one basis or as part of a group. His favourite form of sexual release was to be masturbated by a bikini-clad woman. Back at the Dakota, he began masturbating up to twice a day. He kept a written log of his fantasy lovers that included Yoko's sister Setsuko, Paul's step sister Ruth and oddly, Barbara Walters.

The first public appearance of John and Yoko after their reunion was at the 1975 Grammy Awards on 1 March. John had been invited to present an award with Paul Simon and was photographed with Yoko backstage. At the after party, at the club Les Jardins, John meet up with David Bowie who he had also presented an award at the Grammies. John had met David before and appeared on his album Young Americans. Near the end of the night, Lennon and Bowie went missing. Yoko couldn't find her husband anywhere and sent music publicist Tony King in search of him but it was photographer Bob Gruen who found him. Bob was stood in the hallway when someone opened the door to the women's bathroom. Under one of the cubicles Bob noticed three pairs of cowboy boots that he recognised-they were David Bowie's, John Lennon's and a limo driver's. John, I'm Only Dancing indeed. What was happening between those three men in that toilet cubicle remains a mystery to this day but it wouldn't be the only time David Bowie was caught in suspicious circumstances with a fellow rock star. According to his ex-wife, Angie, she walked in on her husband and Mick Jagger naked in bed together in 1973. David had come out of the closet the year before when he told Melody Maker interviewer Michael Watts, "I'm gay and always have been, even when I was David Jones." At the time David was married to model and actress Angela Barnett, who he had met in 1969 and married the following year. He later joked that he and his wife-to-be had first met while 'fucking the same bloke' and in 1976 he told Playboy "It's true—I am a bisexual".

In the summer of 1975, John meet up with May Pang once again. He hadn't seen her since April, when she left for a temporary job at London's Apple offices. A friend of May's and John's, Richard Ross, was undergoing treatment for Hodgkin's disease at Mount Sinai Hospital and both May and John were paying him a visit. As soon as Richard left the room to visit the bathroom, the two ex-lovers jumped into the sick man's bed and quickly made love before he returned. Even after Sean's birth on 9 October (John's 35th birthday) the Lennons' sex life was all but dead. In October 1976, John took a trip to Hong Kong and later Bangkok. In Bangkok he stayed at the Oriental Hotel, which was situated close by to the city's red light district. Women would hold up cards with numbers on and wait to be ordered like food in a restaurant. Thrown back to his Hamburg days, John was like a child in a candy store. Every night he would pick two or three girls and sometimes the odd Thai boy would be added to his order. John would pay the low prices and lead them back to his hotel room where he would enjoy orgies night after night.

John's affairs continued throughout the 1970s and one night in early 1979, he spent a night of passion with Jo Jo Laine, the wife of Wings guitarist Denny Laine. Jo Jo had first met John Lennon drinking in La Fortuna-a coffee shop on Columbus Avenue in New York. She introduced herself and they got talking.

When she went to leave, John invited her for a drink later that night, she agreed and they met at seven. When a fan spotted them together he asked John who the woman was. John replied she was his bodyguard. The couple enjoyed dinner together at a local Szechuan restaurant. "Halfway through the meal he took my hand and the electricity flowed" Jo Jo remembers. John told Jo Jo that he had the keys to a friend's loft apparent and that the friend was away on tour. After the meal the couple left the restaurant hand in hand and made their way to the apartment. "We wasted no time on preliminaries" Jo Jo remembers. The couple began kissing and "John proved amazingly gentle and patient as he undressed me". John too undressed and purred as Jo Jo stroked her hands across his chest and legs. "Whether it was out of some quirky allegiance to Yoko or what, I quickly sensed it wasn't intercourse he wanted" recalls Jo Jo. She gave him a blowjob "and before the end of the night, a second". Once the couple were redressed, John picked up a guitar and played Jo Jo a song he had written with Harry Nilsson called 'Mucho Mango'. They spent the rest of the night snorting cocaine and talking before Jo Jo got a cab home.

By 1980, Yoko hadn't slept with her husband for years and according to John Green, a tarot-card reader hired by the Lennons in 1974, Yoko would hired prostitutes to satisfy her husband's sexual cravings. Yoko denied the claims saying her sex life with John was very ordinary. But nothing in the life of John and Yoko was very ordinary.

In June 1980, John took a trip to Bermuda where he would write most of the songs that made up his final album Double Fantasy. John's absence was the perfect time for Yoko to begin her affair with Sam Green. One night, Yoko and Sam entertained John Cage and Merce Cuningham at supper and Yoko introduced Sam as her new boyfriend, which was news to Sam. The next day, Yoko came on strong to her employee. Sam rejected all of Yoko's advances but Yoko insisted that the couple should sleep together. Her actions reflected those of John with May Pang a few years previously. "She harangued me" Sam remembers. Yoko sent hours trying to talk Sam into sleeping with her. Eventually, at four in the morning, Sam gave in "my resistance was nil" he said looking back. The next day, Sam had breakfast with Yoko and Sean before leaving.

Despite his resistance, the affair continued and the couple were spotted holding hands at The Tavern on the Green, one of John's favourite restaurants in New York. They spent time in Tampa where they visited a well-known psychic, Leonard Zemke, who Yoko informed that she and Sam were meant to be together for life. On returning to New York, they drove out to Cannon Hall where they had sex for a second time. Fred Seaman witnessed the couple at Cannon Hall and remembers "the two of them disappeared upstairs for some time and then Sam Green came panting down the stairs, his normally neat clothing in disarray". Sam's attitude towards the affair soon changed and for a while Yoko moved in with him at his house on Fire Island. While there, Yoko began to write new material which would later be included on Double Fantasy. Among the new songs was 'Yes, I'm Your Angel' a song she had written for her new lover. The line in the song that refers to a birthday is a message to Sam, whose birthday was 20 May. Yoko was in love and once again she was planning to divorce John Lennon.

Paul and Linda's marriage, on the other hand, had a fairy tale image, with the couple never spending a night apart until 1980 when Paul was arrested in Japan. Paul became the third Beatle to be busted for drugs in 1972. John had been the first when he was arrested in 1968 for possession of hashish. George was next and after a raid on his home in 1969, he was charged with possession of cannabis and fined £250. In 1972, Paul was fined £1,000 for cannabis possession by a Swedish court and later that year police found marijuana plants growing on his farm in Scotland and he was fined £100. He was arrested again in Los Angeles in 1975 for marijuana possession but Linda took the blame. Then, in 1980, he was arrested in Japan after around 200 grams of cannabis was found in his luggage. Linda couldn't take the blame this time and Paul was sent to a Japanese prison for ten days. This was the first and last time Paul and Linda spent any time apart since their marriage in 1969. Linda even went on tour with her husband, bringing the kids along with her. She joined his band, Wings, playing keyboards and providing backing vocals. Paul wrote song after song for Linda including 'Maybe I'm Amazed', 'Long Haired Lady', 'I Am Your Singer', and 'My Love', among others. Their third and final child together, James Louis McCartney was born on 12 September 1977. It seemed as if Paul and Linda were the romance of the century but in reality, not everything was what it seemed. Since her death from cancer in 1998, a handful of Linda's friends have come followed and claimed that Linda was not always happy in her marriage to Paul.

While working on her cookery book, Linda McCartney's Home Cooking, in 1989, with literary agent Peter Cox, Linda gave some interviews in which she not only discussed her recipes but her marriage to Paul. 19 tapes were made in total and according to Peter, the tapes are 'dynamite'. Peter claims that the through of leaving Paul had crossed Linda's mind several times but she had immediately rejected it, her family were the most important thing in her life and she wasn't going to give them up. During the low moments in their marriage Linda felt trapped and according to her friends the McCartneys' marriage was all about Linda making Paul happy. She would mother him, pander to his every whim, dropping everything to be with him when he so demanded it.

Paul could be tight with his money and Peter Cox remembers he often had to lend Linda money for groceries. He also recalls one of Linda's birthdays, when Paul gave her a Cartier watch and made a big deal of making sure she knew how much it was worth. Paul was self-absorbed, arrogant and prone to black moods. He could be short tempered and sometime even violent. Heather Mills, Paul's second wife, had claimed that Paul even once admitted to hitting Linda "once or twice". She went on to claim that she owns a tape recording of Paul talking about his marriage to Linda in which he admits to hitting his first wife. According to Heather, the tape was made with Paul's full knowledge but this seems unlikely. A more likely scenario is that the tape, if it exists at all, was hidden in a handbag.

Despite their ups and downs, Paul stayed forever faithful to Linda throughout their marriage. He often resisted temptation and one example of Paul's loyalty occurred in the early '80s. For his fortieth birthday in 1982, Paul spent the day at Elstree Film Studios recording the music video to accompany his latest single, 'Take It Away'. During a break for lunch Paul was stopped in his tracks by a young women who turned out to be a strippogram by the name of Susie Silvey. Susie had originally intended to do a singing telegram for Paul but when a friend dared her to make it a striptease too she couldn't resist. Dressed in fishnets, suspenders and a black-lace corset under a dress "I could easily peel off when the moment came" Susie turned up unexpected at the studio just before lunch. "I was shaking like a leaf" she remembers and the moment came when Paul left the set for lunch. Susie ran after him and shouted "Paul!" He spun around and as he did she began her striptease as he looked on. After, she sang a "special version of 'All You Need Is Love'" before giving him a birthday congratulations telegram. According to Susie, Paul "thought it was amazing" but unlike the Paul of old he took it no further and Susie got dressed and left.

On 8 December 1980, John Lennon was shot dead outside the Dakota apartment building in New York by crazed Beatles fan Mark David Chapman. Shortly after his death, rumours spread that his widow Yoko Ono had remarried in secret. Her new husband, according to the media, was Hungarian-American interior designer Sam Havadtoy. Yoko first met Sam shortly after her husband's death when she went to a Fifth Avenue interior designers. Yoko hired the 28-year-old to decorate her New York apartment in 1981, and her Palm Beach mansion in 1982. With his long hair, beak-like nose and thick rimmed glasses, Sam was the perfect replacement for John. In 1981, Yoko took a trip to Budapest, Hungary. While there she told the press that Sam Havadtoy was her manager and being from Hungarian origins he had encouraged her to visit his native country. The press began to link their names romantically and in October 1982, reports suggested that a marriage was imminent. Sam's friend and associate, Kerry Westrookes, was reported on saying "Sam says the wedding is definitely on. He is more open about the relationship than Yoko". Rumours about the couple being married continued to spread but in 1986 Yoko denied the rumours saying "He (Sam) has been very caring and he has been good for my son Sean. But we have no plans to get married at this stage." In 1990, Sam also denied the rumours of marriage but not the relationship saying "We're happy. We're living together, boyfriend and girlfriend, yes". The couple split up in 2001.

Meanwhile, John's first wife, Cynthia, had remarried several times after their divorce. She married her second husband, Italian hotelier Roberto Bassanini, in August 1970. The couple had been dating since Cynthia's divorce from John but their marriage didn't last long and they divorced in 1973. In 1976, she married for a third time when she married John Twist, an engineer from Lancashire. Their marriage lasted until 1981, when the couple separated and finally divorced in 1983. During her separation from John Twist she began a relationship with Liverpudlian chauffeur Jim Christie. The couple were together for 17 years before separating in 1998. In 2002, she married once again. This time the groom was night club owner, Noel Charles who passed away in 2013.

Pattie Boyd and Eric Clapton's marriage wasn't running smoothly and during the 1980s Eric had a number of affairs. Among his many women were Rosanne Cash (Johnny's daughter), Paula Yates, and Davina McCall. One affair with studio sound assistant Yvonne Kelly in 1985 resulted in the birth of a daughter, Ruth. His next affair with Italian actress Lory Del Santo resulted in the birth of a son, Conor, in 1986. Pattie and Eric divorced in 1988. Pattie went on to have a fourteen year love affair with property developer Rod Weston. Eric went on to have a number of girlfriends including Patsy Kensit, Naomi Campbell, Sharon Stone and Sheryl Crow before marrying Melia McEnery in 2001. They have had three children together. George would get his revenge on Eric in 1991. George and Eric toured Japan together in December 1991 and during a break in the tour George had a three-day long affair with Eric's then girlfriend Lory Del Santo. The tour came to Hiroshima on 6 December and the band moved into Sun Plaza Hotel. For three days Lory and George locked themselves in George's room but Lory remembers "It was not all about sex". They spent a lot of time talking and one day George arranged for the hotel's pool to be closed off so he and Lory could spend time alone. "In the pool, he was so sweet, he kept massaging my feet" Lory said decades later.

George Harrison's second wife, Olivia Trinidad Arias, was working as a secretary in the Dark Horse Records offices in Los Angeles when she first met George in 1974. George had recently separated from Pattie Boyd but their divorce wouldn't be finalised until 1977. Despite being married, George began a number of different relationships but the most intense of these was with 26-year-old Olivia Arias. Born in Mexico City on 18 May 1948, Olivia grew up in California and while working for Dark Horse Records she would receive daily phone calls from George. Eventually, George sent a friend to

L.A to check her out. He wanted to see if she was as beautiful as she sounded on the phone. She was and when George finally met Olivia in person it was love at first sight. She accompanied him on his Dark Horse tour in 1974 and the couple took a holiday to Hawaii. After the holiday, Olivia moved in with George at Friar Park. In 1977, after spending Christmas in England, the couple moved to George's mansion in Beverly Hills. In December, Olivia announced she was pregnant and a son, Dhani, was born on 1 August 1978. George and Olivia married a month later in a private ceremony at the Henley-on-Thames Register Office in England. The wedding was announced to the press five days later and the couple went on their honeymoon in Tunisia.

Just like in his first marriage, George would have a number of affairs and during the filming of Shanghai Surprise in 1986, rumours spread that George was having an affair with the film's star Madonna despite the presence of her then husband, Sean Penn, on the film's set. Other rumours spread romantically linking George and a young employee of Handmade Films, the film production and distribution company founded by George and his partner Denis O'Brien in 1978. On 30 December 1999, George was attacked in his home by mental ill man, Michael Abram, who believed he was on a mission from God. He believed Paul McCartney was a witch and that George was 'the phantom menace-the alien from Hell'. Abram broken into Friar Park and attacked George with a kitchen knife, puncturing a lung and causing head injuries which later put him in hospital. George was saved by Olivia, who attacked Abram with a poker and then a lamp. George suffered from more than 40 stab wounds but survived the attack. Sadly, in 2001, he died of cancer at the age of 58.

Ringo Starr met his second wife, Barbara Bach on the set of the film Caveman in 1980. Born in Queens on 27 August 1947, Barbara Goldbach was never a fan of The Beatles when growing up. She had attended their 1965 Shea Stadium concert but only to chaperone her younger sister. Barbara much preferred Ray Charles and Bob Dylan. Like Nancy Lee Andrews, Barbara was an Eileen Ford model in her teens. She met Italian businessman Augusto Gregorini in 1965 and they married in 1968. They had two children together, Francesca (born 1968) and Gianni (born in 1972) but they divorced in 1978. Barbara starred in Italian films such as The Sensual Man and The Anonymous Avenger. She moved back to America in 1975 and starred in the James Bond film The Spy Who Loved Me. In 1980, she was cast in Caveman and first met Ringo on the set in Mexico. By March 1980, Ringo had left Nancy Lee Andrews and was now dating Barbara. "I was furious at being abruptly dropped by Ringo for Barbara" Nancy would say later. To begin with, the couple weren't taking things too serious but something changed all that.

On 19 May, Ringo was driving on a wet road in England, when he skidded trying to avoid a truck. His Mercedes crashed into two lampposts before coming to a halt. Ringo was thrown clear, his leg injured, but Barbara was stuck inside. Before help could arrive, Ringo managed to free Barbara and the pair vowed to never part again. Ringo had the car cubed and displayed as a piece of art and a constant reminder of what could have been. Similarly, John and Yoko kept the wreck of the car John crashed in 1969 on display in their garden in Tittenhurst. After the crash, the couple returned to Los Angeles and on the flight over, Ringo proposed. The couple married on 27 April 1981 at Marylebone Register Office in London. (The same venue as Paul and Linda's wedding in 1969.) The wedding was attended by Paul and Linda, George and Olivia, Neil Aspinall, and Derek Taylor, among others. At the reception, held at the club Rag in Mayfair, the three remaining Beatles took part in a jam session along with Ray Cooper and Harry Nilsson.

Ringo had begun drinking heavily in the mid-Seventies after Harry Nilsson introduced him to brandy Alexanders. By the 1980s, he was drinking up to 16 bottles of wine a day. He knew he needed help when he woke up one morning, in 1988, next to a beaten Barbara with no recollection of the events that had taken place the night before. "I'm not a violent man" he told the Express in 2010 "but I was getting violent". Babara was drinking heavily too and the couple booked themselves into a clinic, where they underwent six months of treatment. Once out of rehab, Ringo never drank again.

Winning the second prize for the most hated Beatle

wife is Heather Mills. Born in Aldershot, England in January 1967, her father, John Mills, was a British paratrooper and her mother, Beatrice Mills, was the daughter of a colonel in the British Army. According to her autobiography, Out On a Limb, Heather had lead a very interesting life: She was kidnapped and sexually abused when she was eight, her mother left home when she was nine, her abusive father forced her to shoplift to feed herself, at 15 she ran away and joined a funfair and lived in a cardboard box for four months. Over the years she had worked in several shops and was a waitress for a time.

Heather lost her virginity at sixteen and later said, "Lovemaking was incredible. Sex was everything I'd ever dreamed of." She later claimed that she had had her first orgasm accidently at the age of fifteen while sat in a Jacuzzi. "Once that happened, I was down the squash club every day" she would recall. She moved in with her boyfriend, Stephen, for a while but left him and moved to London. She became a showroom model and travelled to India to try on dress samples before they were mass-produced. By the age of seventeen, she was modelling topless and the next year she set up her own model agency.

In 1987, she moved to Paris and became the mistress of Lebanese millionaire businessman, George Kazan, for two year. During that time she took part in a photo session for the German sex manual Die Freuden der Liebe (The Joys of Love) and also modelled for nude photographs.

In 1989, she moved back to London and married Alfie Karmal, who she had first met before moving to Paris. The marriage didn't last long and after Heather had an affair with her ski instructor, Milos Pagacar, in 1990, the couple divorced in 1991. She next got engaged in 1993 to Raffaele Mincione. That same year she lost her left leg just below the knee after being knocked down by a police motorcycle. She called off her wedding to Raffaele 24 hours before she was due to try on her wedding dress. Within days, she was dating Marcus Stapleton, a tennis tournament organiser and claiming to be "madly, madly in love" with him. That wasn't to last and that same year she was engaged to TV director Chris Tertill, who she planned to marry in August but by the end of the year she had called it off.

Heather Mills first met Paul McCartney in 1999, when they both appeared at the Pride of Britain Awards on 20 May. During the award ceremony Heather pretended an award and made an appeal on behalf of the Heather Mills Health Trust. "I thought Heather's speech was great" Paul remembered later "it got me thinking." Paul spoke to Heather briefly and in October he donated £150,000 to her charity. Paul was impressed by Heather's work and found her number. He rang her to talk about the charity but, "I realised I fancied her". The pair began meeting regularly to discuss Heather's charity work but by November they were an item. They first slept together on the night of 5 November at Paul's home in Sussex. That same month Paul added backing vocals to the charity single, 'VO!CE', that Heather had recorded with her sister, Fiona, which was released on Coda records. Paul and Heather first appeared in public together in 2000, at Heather's 32nd birthday party. The couple began being seen at events together, and they went on several holidays, including a trip to India and in 2001, a holiday in the Lake District where, on 23 July, Paul proposed and presented her with a £150,000 diamond and sapphire ring. They married a year later, on 11 June 2002, at Castle Leslie in the Irish village of Glaslough. Paul was 59, Heather was 33 but had been reported as saying "It doesn't even bother me that he's much older than me." The song 'Heather' from the 2001 album Driving Rain was played during the ceremony. Guests included Ringo and his wife Barbara, and George Martin among other celebrity friends. On their wedding night the couple slept in separate rooms in the castle.

The fans and Paul's family alike were unhappy. Paul's children went public with their dislike for Heather, who they thought was a gold-digger and the public agreed. After the wedding, Heather was attacked by the British press but Paul wouldn't listen and the couple honeymooned in the Seychelles. Most of the honeymoon was spent making love and the public were shocked in 2003 when the couple announced that Heather was pregnant. On 28 October 2003, a daughter, Beatrice Milly McCartney, was born. Heather had suffered previous ectopic pregnancies before meeting Paul and a miscarriage in the first year of their marriage.

Despite an active sex life, Heather complained to friends saying Paul was a "boring old fart". By 2005, Paul and Heather's marriage was falling apart with more frequent arguments that on occasion would lead to violent outbursts by Paul. Leaked divorce documents would revile that Paul would often become drunk and violet towards his wife, during one incident he pushed her over a coffee table and another time he pushed her into a bath. The couple separated in May 2006 and after a lengthy court battle, the pair divorced in 2008. The press and the public alike hated Heather and the media couldn't wait to dish the dirt on her, giving her the nickname Lady Mucca. They saw her as nothing more than a gold-digger that had somehow wormed her way into the heart and wallet of England's most cherished icon.

By the time the divorce was granted, Paul was already dating another woman. His relationship with Nancy Shevell began in November 2007 and the couple were seen on dates together, visiting restaurants and watching baseball matches as well as taking several holidays together. The reaction to Nancy was the complete opposite to what it had been to Heather. Nancy was a millionaire New Yorker who was born in 1960 into a wealthy family and so neither Paul nor his children had to worry about her being a gold-digger. She first married a lawyer, Bruce Blakeman, in 1985 and the couple had a son togther, Arlen Blakeman, who was born in 1992. Nancy and Bruce divorced in 2008. Paul had been seen around town with a number of other women including actress Rosanna Arquette, former Olympic horse-rider Tanya Larrigan, Australian model Elle Macpherson, Sabrina Guinness who once dated Prince Charles, American actress Renee Zellweger, and American model Christie Brinkley. But it was Nancy who won Paul's heart and they became engaged in May 2011 and married later that year on what would have been John Lennon's 71st birthday-9 October 2011. The ceremony took place at Old Marylebone Town Hall, where Paul and Linda had married in 1969 and Ringo and Barbara had married in 1981. Paul wrote the song 'My Valentine' for his new wife and the song was played at the wedding. It was later included on the 2012 album Kisses on the Bottom. The wedding guests included Ringo and Baraba and all of the McCartney children. Son, James, was best man while Paul's youngest daughter, Beatrice, was a flower girl. The wedding dress was designed by Paul's second daughter Stella and his oldest daughter, Mary, was the official photographer. A reception was held at Paul's home in St. John's Wood and guest included Olivia Harrison and Pattie Boyd.

Paul has had so many women over the years but admits he still finds it hard to say those three little words. On a hidden track, 'Scared', on his latest album, New, he sings "I'm scared to say 'I love you'" to his third wife Nancy. But for now, at least, it seems Paul has found his happy ending.

12

Was John Lennon Gay?

Whenever discussing the relationship between John Lennon and The Beatles' manager Brian Epstein the same question is always asked. While writing this book that question crept up time and time again. Was John Lennon gay? To give the short answer, no, he wasn't, but like a lot of things in Lennon's life, his sexuality is far more complex than that. Many people have tried to unravel the secrets of John Lennon's sexuality. One argument is that not only was John not gay but he was homophobic. This argument comes from that fact that John could be cruel towards gay men, especially Brian Epstein, and would use homophobic terms and insults. I have never met John Lennon so I cannot say for sure whether he was or wasn't homophobic. What I can do however is give evidence that he wasn't.

John knew and was friends with many openly gay or bisexual men including David Bowie, Elton John, Andy Warhol, and Brian Epstein. When he was asked in 1972 to contribute something to the gay liberation book, he was more than happy to donate a sketch of a male nude sat on a flying carpet shouting: 'Why make it sad to be gay? Doing your thing is OK. Our body's our own so leave us alone. Go play with yourself-today!' In March 1975, John created a collage for Elton John's birthday. The collage shows images of muscular men, penises, a horse, and Elton himself as well as one photo of John. John obviously loved his friend to take time to make him a collage for his birthday. These are not the actions of a homophobic man and John's homophobic behaviour towards people like Brian Epstein was most likely the result of his working-class background. If anything, John was afraid that he might be homosexual himself. When asked about his beating of Bob Wooler he remarked "I had a fear that maybe I was homosexual to attack him like that. It's very complicated reasoning."

The biggest argument against John being gay is not whether he was homophobic or not it is his sexual relationships with women. For most of his adult life, John Lennon was a married man. He married Cynthia Powell in 1962 and was married to her until 1968. In 1969, he married Yoko Ono, who was his wife up until his death in 1980. You could argue that his marriages were a way to mask his true sexuality but then what of his numerous affairs with women? If John was secretly gay why would he bother having secret affairs with women? He won't. John loved women and straight sex. There is no doubt John Lennon was sexually attracted to the female form. Throughout his life, John slept with hundreds of women. There is tons of evidence to back up that claim. Most of it is in this book. These are not the actions of a homosexual man despite how much he may want to keep his sexuality a secret. We know for a fact that Brian Epstein was a closeted homosexual but he didn't go to any great effort to keep it a secret, he didn't marry and didn't have girlfriends, so it seems silly to even suggest the John would go to extremes to hide his own sexuality.

There is no doubt that John Lennon was not a homosexual so why then are we discussing it here oppose to say discussing whether or not Paul McCartney, George Harrison, or Ringo Starr were gay. The answer is simple; there is no evidence or in fact any rumours that the other Beatles may have been gay and it's not for lack of looking that I didn't come across any rumours that claim any of the other Beatles were gay and why would there be? They were all straight men, who married women and had girlfriends. In a dark corner of the internet, I did find one rumour about a man that may or may not have been Paul McCartney having a one off gay encounter with another unknown man but the information was so vague that-if it was true at all-it could have easily been anyone. No names, no location and no date was given so there was no reason to not dismiss it as BS. The only other thing I could find as 'evidence' that Paul was gay is that he wrote the song 'Michelle'. To the English listener it appears to be a French sounding song about a woman named Michelle but in France it sounds as if Paul is singing about a man named Michel, the French equivalent to the English name Michael. This is nonsense of course because Michelle is a French name too and is the feminine form of Michael. As wonderful as the internet is, it is equally strange and one should not linger there. But what about Ringo? Didn't he sing 'Boys'? Paul explains:

"It was really a girls' song. 'I talk about boys now!' Or it was a gay song. But we never listened. It's just a great song. I think that's one thing about youth-you just don't give a shit. I love the innocence of those days."

The lyrics of the song specifically talk about boys kissing girls and not each other and was a favourite among the bands playing in Liverpool at the time. The Pete Best Combo even recorded a version in 1965 so there!

What makes John any different from his fellow band mates? Well there is evidence and rumours to suggest that John Lennon had sexual relationships with other men. A quick internet search will prove that. So why do these stories exist? You could argue that these stories only came to light after John's death and that's why there isn't similar stories about any of the other Beatles but that just wouldn't be true. Rumours about John's sexuality have been circulating since 1963. Besides, George Harrison died in 2001 and no similar stories about his sexuality have come to light.

If John Lennon was not homosexual was he bisexual? There is enough evidence to suggest that he was. I have discussed most of this evidence elsewhere in this book so I will simply reference them here and give page numbers for each piece of evidence.

- As a teenager John enjoyed taking part in mutual masturbation sessions with his male friends (Pages 25-26)
- John received oral sex from a transvestite in Hamburg (Page 65)
- John gave oral sex to Stuart Sutcliffe in Hamburg (Pages 57-58)
- John had a sexual relationship with Brian Epstein (Pages 104-108, 146)
- John had a sexual experience with Royston Ellis (Pages 121-122)
- John had a gay experience with a man in 1965 (Page 159-160)
- John took part in muti-gender orgies (Page 159)
- John made sexual advances on a male fan (Pages 230-231)
- John kissed Jesse Ed Davis (Page 228)
- John had a sexual experience with David Bowie (Page 234)

Another story that sticks out when discussing John Lennon's sexuality took place one night in 1967. John and his friend Pete Shotton had been dropping acid at John's house in Kenwood. As the night came to an end, the two men found themselves in John's attic where they eventually passed out, almost literally laying on top of each other. The next morning, John woke up to the sound of his maid making her way to the attic. He shot up saying "Oh Christ, she'll think we've been fucking". Why would the maid jump to such a conclusion unless she knew a secret? Had she walked in on John and one of his male lovers before? All this evidence seems to suggest that John Lennon was bisexual. You could argue that John was not bisexual but was a sexual explorer, who would try anything at least once but I would strongly disagree. There are far too many incidents to suggest that John was simply experimenting. I'll leave the last words to Tony Manero, who, when he was questioned about the reality of his story, had this to say "John did come on to me. He did try to make love to me. He asked me to perform a lewd act and that's the truth. The man was bisexual. There are no two ways about it."

Special Thanks

The author would like to thank the following people:

First and foremost my parents, Margaret and Duncan without whom.....

And my two sisters, Zoe and Natasha. Angie Bourke-the best friend and business partner a boy could wish for. Max Gibbons-a true friend, mate, buddy, and pal, who one day will be able to read for himself. Kate Hole-a loyal friend, companion and teacher. My three strong, beautiful women, Tara Sharlotte, Rani Tara-Chan and Leanne Wood, who have shown love and support throughout. Pete Nash-who gave me my first break and helped shed light on darker areas of Beatledom. Kate Mossman for legal advice and Gemma Morton for help with the cover art.

And of course, John, Paul, George and Ringo who kept the sixties well and truly swinging.

Sorry, nobody could be bothered with an index.